A SONG I HEARD THE OCEAN SING

A SONG I HEARD THE *Ocean Sing*

LAURA MANSFIELD

WordCrafts Press

"
I must be
a mermaid, Rango.
I have no fear of depths and
a great fear of shallow living.
"

Anaïs Nin

For Bill, who first believed in me

CHAPTER 1

The thumbtacked picture showed a weathered, white-shingled house with sea-green shutters and a slate-grey tin roof. Another image showed a comfortably saggy back porch that faced the ocean. There was a porch swing, painted the palest shade of blue, like the sky over the sea on an ordinary day. It wasn't the piercing cerulean of October skies, just a soft, broken-in color, like old blue jeans. There were some faded ticking-striped pillows tucked in the corner of the swing to soften its edges. Really, it was the porch swing that spoke to Alice. *Come sit and rock and read and relax. Watch the waves. Let the sounds of the sea hypnotize you and lull you into actual contentment,* it whispered.

Was it really that simple? Alice wondered. Something about that swing and those pillows comforted her. Reminded her of her grandmother. Her childhood. Even though her grandmother had lived in a regular neighborhood nowhere near the beach. And Alice had never had a house with a porch swing.

She tore off one of the dangling strips of phone numbers. And six weeks later here she was.

Alice had led an eventful, if not an extraordinary life. All that was about to change.

As she gazed out the window of the endearingly shabby beach house, she wondered what was next and whether it was finally *her* turn. Her turn to star in her own life. She was coming off a disastrous, albeit brief, second marriage to a misogynistic narcissist.

She'd been shaken to her very core. Had caved in on herself and crawled back out again. She had raised her beautiful, brilliant, brave boy Scott and seen him fly the nest. Literally. He'd joined the Air Force. She had cared lovingly for her aging parents and dutifully dispatched them to the Pearly Gates. She had worked for twenty-five years at a series of demanding executive jobs.

So, she wondered if, in fact, it *was* her turn.

Even the thought felt naughty and selfish. *You don't get a turn, Alice. Yours is a life of service and duty and dinner parties and Depends and conference calls and soccer games.* Her inner voice taunted her. *The very idea. You don't get to go on a vision quest or have a sweat-lodge epiphany. You're not going to find yourself. Your Kundalini isn't going to rise. None of that New Age bullshit.*

Alice shook the negative self-talky cobwebs away and said out loud, "Why not?"

After all, she had taken the first step on a journey of self-discovery. She'd sold her comfy cottage in the suburbs, invested prudently, and passed on her family treasures, the few that remained from the ruins of her previous life. Then she'd Googled beach houses, culling through vacation rentals and Airbnbs, not at all sure what she was looking for, but confident she'd know it when she found it. Turns out it wasn't online but on the community bulletin board at the local Piggly Wiggly where she found her future.

The place smelled pleasantly musty when she arrived, fresh sheets and towels in Target bags slung over her arms. Everything else was already there. The house was sparsely furnished, but Alice didn't need much. She was entering a minimalist phase of her life. Stripping away the non-essentials. The hardwood floors were worn but clean and recently refinished. There was a fresh coat of cloud-white paint on all the walls. An old-fashioned claw-footed tub in the single bathroom. And that beguiling porch swing that even now was beckoning Alice, as she scrubbed the sink and mopped the kitchen floor. Not that anything was dirty. It was just her way of feeling at home, making the space her own. The scent of Murphy's Oil Soap soothed her.

Alice paused, with her rubber-gloved hands immersed in hot

suds, breathed in the tangy salt air and stared out the window at the sea. It was mesmerizing. Her place was at the end of the beach, away from the hotels and multi-storied high-end rentals on stilts. Her view was of driftwood in peculiar shapes, washed ashore and left to weather and morph with the seasons. If you squinted, it looked like a fanciful collection of writhing beasts, dragons perhaps, or little Loch Ness monsters. Alice approved. She fully supported a deserted beach that wasn't manicured and swept. That didn't have wooden lounge chairs with matching umbrellas dotting the sand. Just a sculpture garden of things coughed up by the sea.

"And now," cried Max, *"let the wild rumpus start."*

Alice could close her eyes and populate her driftwood tableau with the boy wearing a crown and a wolf suit, frolicking with his fanciful creatures in Maurice Sendak's beloved picture book. She'd read it aloud to Scott till the pages wore thin. She'd read it to herself as a child.

"There should be a place where only the things you want to happen, happen."

Summer was officially over. Labor Day Weekend had come and gone. Schools were back in session. Tourists had headed home to their real lives. And jobs. And deadlines. And responsibilities. Sun-kissed and salty, sand still in their shoes.

That's why Alice was so surprised to see a little girl darting among the driftwood dragons.

Alice blinked and tried to rouse herself from her daydream.

She looked over her shoulder to see Tabitha, her feline familiar, tiptoeing gingerly but intentionally across the freshly mopped kitchen floor, leaving little sandy paw prints as she went. Alice smiled and talked in her special cat voice to the yellow-eyed tabby she'd found in a McDonald's dumpster thirteen years ago. Stray cats were hearty and self-reliant. And street-smart and resilient. Alice knew Tabitha could make the transition from snoozing in suburban sun puddles to chasing sand crabs. She was right on all accounts. Tabitha seemed at home and entirely unfazed by her new surroundings. She didn't wander far from her food bowl, which sat in the corner of the kitchen near the back door. The screen on the door was conveniently torn so Tabitha had only to pop her head through to get in and out. It fell back in place behind her like a rusty metal curtain.

When Alice looked back out the window, there was no one there.

Alice's to-do list was short and sweet: visit the local bookstore and find a good yoga studio. She hadn't thought beyond that. She had signed a six-month lease with an option to renew. The property was owned by a couple back in Alice's hometown. Their kids were grown, and they now preferred the mountains to the ocean. Didn't want to sell the place just yet and were happy to have a responsible, reliable adult keeping an eye on things. Particularly in the off-season. Single-family rentals weren't in great demand, at least not ones this small. The trend was toward big houses where extended families and wedding parties could gather barefoot, in matching white outfits for sunset pictures that would later become Christmas cards. That was all on the other end of the island.

Alice wasn't worried about being bored. Or getting lonely. In fact, she craved the solitude and the quiet after her hectic and harried life back home. She planned to read and cook and write letters. She envisioned meandering walkabouts on the beach followed by catnaps and long floaty baths. There was no TV in the cottage, and the wi-fi was abysmal. Alice was giddily off the grid.

She loved the unhurried pace of island life. Perpetual vacation mode. Now that the summer crowds had dwindled, it was easy to get around. She could ride her bicycle to the cluster of shops and restaurants in the center of town. There was no need to drive unless she wanted more groceries than she could fit in the rickety wicker basket attached to the rusty bike she had bought from the island rental shop. They had been only too happy to give her a good price on the beaten-up cruiser and free up some space for next season's newer models. Alice thought the battered bike had charm and sort of went with the cottage like a vintage handbag with a favorite pair of red tag Levi's. The bell on the handlebar made a satisfyingly scritchy *clang-clang*.

So, it came to be that Alice found herself on a Tuesday morning in The Beachcomber, the only grocery store on the island, which was a delightful mix of locally grown produce and suntan lotions, freshly caught seafood and tacky T-shirts. She was happily lost in the tomatoes, the last of the season, still warm from the sun. Plump, straining against their skins. There was a wonderful selection of heirlooms—yellow tomatoes and green ones with names like Sunny Boy and Green Zebra and an unusual purple variety Alice had never seen before. "Purple Skye" said the little hand-written sign by the crate.

"Those taste like sunshine," offered a pleasant baritone voice over Alice's shoulder as she gently touched the gorgeous purplish-brown tomatoes. "With plummy overtones."

The voice was Sam Elliott-esque, gravelly and sonorous. But also, slightly Southern.

"You make it sound like wine," Alice mused. "Wonder if they have tomato tastings and pairings here."

"They're perfect in a salad with olive oil and rosemary-infused vinegar," said the man of indeterminate age. He had nice crow's feet and laugh lines and dimples. Was tall with salt and pepper in his dark blonde hair and chocolate eyes. Tanned but not like he'd been trying.

"I'm Finn, by the way. And I grow these little beauties."

Alice looked from Finn to the tomatoes and back again. He looked like that Danish actor who played Jaime Lannister on "Game of Thrones." Nikolaj something. She bet people told him that all the time and resolved on the spot not to. She didn't trust handsome men.

She had a momentary flashback to watching all eight seasons of *GoT* with Scott before he shipped out. It was their thing, and he humored her instinctive reactions to the sword fights and sudden, gory deaths, the court drama and intrigue told against a sweeping backdrop of fire and ice. Even the theme song brought tears to her eyes. She gasped involuntarily remembering when Jaime sank into the watery depths at the end of the fourth episode of the seventh season.

Openly weeping into her generous pour of Pinot Grigio as she sat on the sofa, Alice had blubbered, "You know I've always had a secret crush on Jaime."

"I know, and it's not much of a secret," Scott had replied from across the living room where he was multi-screening, laptop and phone balanced on his knees like cyborg extensions of his arms. "Now, shush!"

Alice's history with men was complicated. She was planning a man-free getaway, and here was a hot guy already chatting her up in The Beachcomber. She glanced at his left hand. No ring, but that didn't mean anything. Finn wore a disarmingly bemused expression, as if Alice had just said something clever, and he was in on the joke.

"Hmm …" said Alice, noncommittally. She longed to turn back to the tomatoes and ignore him. But thinking she needed to befriend the locals, she smiled instead and said, "I'm Alice."

They small-talked about the weather and tomatoes. Then Finn cocked his head to one side and grinned crookedly as though he knew more about Alice than he should. Like he wanted to say something else but didn't. He tossed a tomato and caught it over-handed like a baseball snatched in midair. With his left hand. Alice had a soft spot for lefties. Finn dropped the tomato gently back in the crate and ambled away, leaving Alice where he'd found her.

"See you around, Alice."

Back at the cottage, Alice opened a bottle of grocery-store Sau Blanc, the label had seashells on it, so it seemed appropriate. She sipped as she stirred extra-virgin olive oil and balsamic vinegar with a dollop of Dijon mustard in the bottom of a cracked wooden bowl. She ground fresh peppercorns on top, enjoying the satisfying crackle the pepper grinder made with each emphatic twist. Alice washed and sliced one perfectly ripe purple tomato and tossed it with field greens and shitake mushrooms. Crumbled some lovely Roquefort cheese on top and took her salad and wine out to the porch swing. Almost as an afterthought she grabbed a sprig of rosemary from the sunbaked clay container on the porch and sheared the fragrant needles with her fingers directly onto her salad. Absentmindedly, Alice ran her herb-seasoned hands through her tousled honey-blonde hair as she settled into the swing and tucked into her salad.

She savored the pungent taste of the tomatoes as the flavors burst in her mouth. "Purple Skye," Alice said aloud to herself, rocking back and forth with her bare feet scooting against the faded barn-red floorboards of the porch. A windchime made of sea glass clattered softly in the breeze that blew in from the ocean, carrying with it the familiar smells of salt and sunshine, promise and possibility.

As she watched the sun set over the ocean, slipping into the sea like a giant orange lollipop, Alice was reminded of another sunset over 3,000 miles away.

She had always been charmed by the legend of the Faerie Flag that hung over Dunvegan Castle in ancient times on the Isle of Skye. Now a framed faded shred of silk, the banner, likely made in Syria and brought back during the Crusades, had never burned even when the castle caught fire.

Alice and Scott visited the fabled fortress, the MacLeod family seat for over 800 years, and her ancestral home on her mother's side. It's the oldest continuously inhabited castle in Scotland, never conquered, never breached. Still *holding fast*, as per the family motto.

They'd been to Skye, off the west coast of Scotland, to scatter her mother's ashes. It had been an adventure, driving across the country in a tiny motorcoach and then taking a ferry to the island with a bunch of strangers, who became fast friends. McClures, of Clan MacLeod, liked to point out that they were *islanders* not *highlanders*.

She and Scott had not ventured down to Loch Dunvegan to visit the famous seal colony, but she imagined selkies, "selkie fowk" in Scots, shedding their seal skins and taking human form to dance on the shore before returning to the icy, black waters.

Alice could still close her eyes and conjure up that magical sunset over Skye, as a lone bagpiper played near the base of Neist

Point Lighthouse. Bagpipes had always pulled Alice's heart into her throat. The mournful, proud notes, wrestled from the sheepskin into the pipes. Such a visceral sound, plaintive and clear and physically wrought. It took powerful lungs and lots of effort to coax the tune out of the strange-looking instrument and release it on the wind. She had hired a bagpiper to play "Amazing Grace" at her mother's funeral back in Georgia the year before. And here a world away, the Scottish piper was playing the same hymn as the sun sank low in the sky, through tiers of burnt orange, deep rose, and finally, purple.

That night after meeting Finn at the grocery store, Alice slept under patchwork quilts she'd found in the linen closet with crumbling sprigs of dried lavender tucked between them. They were well worn, even threadbare in places—reminiscent of Dunvegan's Faerie Flag—and Alice had aired them out all day on the clothesline. The weight of the quilts was comforting. The bed was heaven. She both heard and felt Tabitha's purring presence, a reminder of home, wherever *home* was now. It was more of a concept than an actual place for Alice. She closed her eyes and counted the places she'd lived, the different stages of her life from kissing prom dates under the front porch light of her childhood home to her single-girl apartment with the radiators that hissed and moaned. There was her happily married house with Scott's dad, where she'd watched her toddler son hunt Easter eggs in the front yard. Alice had thought she'd watch her grandchildren do the same. Leaving that house had wrecked her in a way she'd never fully recovered from. It was the ending of everything she'd thought she was supposed to do and be. The death of a dream.

Twenty years later, Alice listened to the tinny vibrations of rain pattering on the roof as she fell asleep in her cozy bed in the little cottage by the sea. Alice dreamed all kinds of things she couldn't remember. She slept hard and awoke with a start, sunlight already streaming through the window, Tabitha mewing impatiently for food and swatting Alice not so gently on the face with her big soft paw. Alice lay still for a moment trying to recapture the wisp of her dreams as they slipped away.

"Okay, kitty britches, let's get you fed," she said at last, scooping up the cat as she climbed out of bed, putting Tabitha over her shoulder like a long-tailed toddler. Alice padded into the kitchen and bustled about, making tea and feeding the cat and doing the multi-tasking morning dance we all do in the privacy of our own kitchens.

"Hello," came a small voice, interrupting Alice's vitamin-te-abag-orange-juice shuffle. Alice looked up with a start, to see a little girl sitting at her breakfast table, coltish brown legs dangling not quite to the floor. Dirty bare feet swinging back and forth, a bracelet of woven seaweed around one delicate ankle.

Alice was speechless. She didn't feel threatened by the child, who couldn't have been more than six or seven years old. But there was something about the girl—besides the fact that she had let herself in and made herself at home in Alice's kitchen. She was tiny and fragile looking but also fierce and confident. Something in her eyes, those exotic eyes, made her seem wise beyond her years. An old soul inhabiting a youthful body. Her hair was wild and wavy and windblown. The color of dune grass bleached by the sun and impossibly tangled in places. She had a feral look about her. Was wearing only faded khaki shorts and a turquoise bikini top, both of which had seen better days. Her clothes were worn but not dirty, Alice noticed, with the trained eye of a mother, who inadvertently scans for skinned knees and missing buttons.

Transfixed, bewitched, Alice was lost in the girl's eyes, which seemed to change colors from sea green to dark navy to the softest shade of blue, the very color of the porch swing and the beach sky. She had ocean eyes.

Tabitha wound herself around the legs of the little girl's chair, undisturbed by the alien being perched above. After making several figure eights, the cat sat serenely on her haunches, licking her paw and washing her face, bending her ear back in the process, so it lay flat against her head, like a crushed pink flower.

"What's your name, sweetie?" Alice managed at last.

"Skye," said the girl.

As improbably as this sounded, Alice accepted Skye's answer, noticing the brown paper bag of tomatoes half spilled out onto the scarred white surface of the round wooden table. The name and price per pound of the luscious love apples written in Sharpie on the outside of the bag.

Alice bustled into mom-mode which meant feeding people, especially children.

"Hmm. Are you hungry, err, Skye?" Alice asked as she uncovered the steel-cut oats that had been cooking overnight on the stovetop. Warm waves of breakfast smells wafted up from the pot. Without waiting for a reply, she scooped a generous portion into one of the mismatched chipped bowls from the cupboard and tossed a handful of blueberries on top for good measure.

Antioxidants, she thought to herself automatically, as she always did with food, mentally chronicling the benefits, as if to justify their consumption. A habit left over from decades of counting calories and rationalizing food choices.

The tiny girl attacked the oatmeal with untamed intensity, holding her spoon caveman style.

Alice sipped her herbal tea and chatted nervously about nothing. She didn't want to spook Skye or scare her somehow. Though the child's physical stature was slight, her presence was powerful. Alice noticed the fine blonde fur on her caramel arms, the delicate sculpted biceps and triceps of a budding ballerina.

Under the table, Tabitha complacently cleaned her claws.

When the bowl was empty, the little girl looked up and stared right into Alice's eyes. They held each other's gaze for a longish moment. There was something familiar about Skye, something Alice couldn't quite place. "Thank you," Skye said softly as she slipped from the chair and darted out the screen door, which slap-slapped gently behind her. Tabitha dashed after her, as though chasing a chipmunk, through the screen and off the porch—bounding silently on velvet paws behind the girl's bare feet.

"But wait," Alice stammered, finally standing up, breaking the spell she'd been under. By the time she got to the door and looked out, Tabitha was sprawled on the porch under the swing, which swayed a little in the breeze. Skye was nowhere to be seen.

Shaking her head, Alice stepped back inside, again doing the autopilot polka of the highly efficient; picking up the bowl, loading the dishwasher, wiping down the table, talking to herself a little, and to Tabitha who had wandered back in. The old cat followed Alice from room to room and made herself at home on the unmade bed while Alice wriggled into her yoga clothes.

As she pedaled down the quiet street in front of the cottage with her yoga mat in its canvas bag slung over her shoulder, she wondered about the little sprite who had joined her for breakfast. Where did she live? Who were her parents? Alice made a mental note to ask around. Maybe someone at the yoga studio would know. Or maybe she'd see the hot tomato guy again. Now she'd have an excuse to talk to him. Then she mentally chastised herself. *What are you thinking? Stop right now. You don't need entanglements. Attachments. Have you learned nothing? Men are for flirtations and fantasies. Not for real-life relationships.*

And on she went, having a lively conversation with herself in her head, until she pulled up to the gravel parking lot of the Laughing Lotus and placed her bike in the rack beside the others. She had noticed the place the other day when she was in town. It had a nice vibe. There was a big colorful mural painted on the side of the building, and the studio opened to the fresh air by way of a glass-paneled garage door. Alice was always immediately at home in yoga studios. The smoldering sage, the Spandex-clad women wearing mala beads and radiant smiles. She felt herself relax as she signed in and put cash in the basket. It was a karma class—a sort of pay-what-you-feel arrangement embraced by trendy, well-intentioned yoga communities, like goat yoga and gongs.

Alice did what she always did during her practice. She went inward, tuning out the chatter around her and surrendering to the ebb and flow of the postures, moving stiffly at first, feeling each ache and pain of her fifty-some-odd years then finally feeling nothing at all. She focused on her breathing, in and out through her nose, and pushed herself into the asanas, unwinding and relaxing. She felt her shoulders unclench and her face soften. Yoga was better than sex as far as Alice was concerned. In fact, she didn't miss sex at all. It was like dessert, delicious if you were in the mood, but nonessential. Yoga, however, was as essential as oxygen.

It was only after a particularly satisfying shavasana, when Alice was gathering up her belongings, that she noticed Finn in the back of the room, rolling up his mat, chatting with a beautiful woman, lissome in her Lululemon, perfectly toned abs on full display between her midriff top and low-rise yoga pants. The neoprene leggings hugged her body and accentuated her curves. Lulu really did do the best yoga pants, Alice had to concede, as she automatically appraised and admired the woman's physique.

When Alice was done mentally comparing herself to the gorgeous yogini, she glanced at Finn who was staring right at her. He did that thing with his chin that her son sometimes did, a sort of greeting/acknowledgment and then he turned and left, following the yoga goddess out of the studio. Had his eyes lingered just a moment on Alice, she wondered? Or had she imagined it. And was he smiling at her or laughing at her?

The days turned into weeks as Alice fell into a comfortable rhythm. Eat, sleep, yoga, repeat. She took long walks on the beach, sometimes Tabitha came with her. They made an improbable duo, Alice striding purposefully, eyes on the sand, always on the lookout for sharks' teeth and pretty shells, Tabitha sauntering, darting, pouncing, then stopping, as cats do, to groom themselves as if on cue. Alice hadn't seen Skye again—the girl, not the tomatoes.

Alice thought she heard soft footfalls on the porch some nights after she'd gone to bed. Sometimes she'd tiptoe out to see, with the light of the full harvest moon overhead, the porch swing gently swaying. There was magic in the air at midnight. The tide was high, and the sea was lively, moving mysteriously to a rhythm all its own. Alice would stand there for a moment, scanning the darkness till her eyes adjusted. The sandy floorboards felt warm and reassuring under her bare feet. But there was no visible sign of the feral faery princess, as Alice had come to think of her.

She hadn't seen Finn again either. She'd gathered from the chatter at the yoga studio that he came and went from Kennesaw Island. That he was an attorney and still had a practice in Atlanta. That he was divorced and had suffered a terrible tragedy no one spoke of. Out of respect or discretion or because it was simply too awful to discuss. Alice wasn't sure which.

One weekend in early October, several of Alice's girlfriends came out to see her and catch up on all the things. She'd been content on her own but was glad for the distraction of wine and women and laughter. These women were Alice's touchstones, her tribe, her family, especially with Scott overseas. Some of their friendships dated to elementary school. Others to high school. Old friends who could pick up the threads of each other's lives across time and space and hold each other safely in acceptance with compassion. They'd grown up and were now growing older together. Sailing through midlife to whatever was waiting on the other side. Wise women bound by a lifetime of trust.

Alice had booked spa treatments for the gaggle at the stately old hotel on the other side of the island. Afterwards, they'd come back to the cottage and taken a pitcher of margaritas to the beach to watch the sun set. Then they stayed up all night talking about their kids, their husbands and "wasbunds"—the term they used for exes. The women finally tumbled into bed, with Alice and on the foldout sofa in the living room. It was like a high-school slumber party, but the dog-eared *Seventeen Magazines* and *Cosmo* quizzes had given way to back issues of *Garden & Gun* and *Southern Living* casserole recipes. Empty wine bottles and glasses were scattered about where cans of Tab would have been. Expensive anti-aging serums and foot creams covered the bathroom counter where Clearasil and Noxzema had kept silent vigil decades ago with hot rollers and Love's Baby Soft.

Alice still dutifully wore her retainer. At least most nights. Some things hadn't changed.

The weekend was one long conversation—a non-stop, pleasantly random discussion of life's little triumphs and tragedies. Alice and her friends would sort through each other's stories, mining for nuggets of universal truth. Picking up on recurring themes from the past 40-plus years.

You've always been too hard on yourself. You're not fat. You look great.

Don't listen to your sister. She's crazy, bless her heart.

Children grow up and leave. That means we've done our jobs right, doesn't it?

They covered it all. Their marriages and the unraveling of some of them. The profound joy and never-ending anxiety of parenting—both their children and now their own parents. Jobs, houses, books, gardening, fashion, politics, gossip about old classmates. How so much had changed and how some things never did.

They shared ancient beauty secrets: *your eyebrows should be twins not sisters.*

There was talk of impending joint surgeries for this group of former athletes, ex-cheerleaders and ladies-league tennis players.

And, of course, the ongoing debate about plastic surgery and whether this was enhancing or betraying one's natural beauty. Should they scorn it or embrace it? Did aging gracefully include scalpels as well as Botox and fillers? And if they chose to follow the wisdom of their shared spirit animal, Dolly Parton—who is said to have said, *if it's saggin', baggin', or draggin', get it nipped, tucked, or sucked*—then when was the right time to make these adjustments?

Other than Beth's lumpectomy scare, their little gang had been remarkably unscathed by serious illness. Until now.

They laughed till they cried when Bekuh said her husband's recently installed pacemaker was making him want sex every night, even after 30 years of marriage. Bekuh was pleasantly exhausted.

Alice reflected on her recent collection of broken boyfriends—survivors from the Island of Misfit Man Toys—tattered Raggedy Andys and wounded G.I. Joes, who in their own emotional anguish had been unable to love completely. Incapable of making a deep soul-to-soul connection. That was the only connection Alice really wanted. She craved depth.

"You always choose men who *hurt* you," blurted Debbie over mimosas Sunday morning. Alice's bestie since ninth grade, Debbie was mostly happily married to a much-older husband. No children of her own, Debbie had thrown herself into her blended family with lots of step-kids and their spouses and their various issues. Alice could never keep them all straight. She wasn't convinced that Debbie could either.

Her old friend's words stung. Was Debbie implying that Alice *chose* to be hurt? That she could see it coming and ran toward the pain? "Always" was a stretch, wasn't it?

"Just be careful with Finn. That's all I'm saying," Debbie added, wrapping Alice in a big, warm, terrycloth-clad hug, as they applied expensive sunscreen to their faces and necks, before heading down to the beach.

"He sounds kinda broken, and you can't keep trying to fix people."

All in all, it was a lovely weekend of feeling connected and content. Alice was grateful to spend time with her small circle of chosen ones. And she was also grateful when they left. Alice was becoming more and more the introvert. Too much people time drained her.

Bekuh took her aside as they packed up their respective SUVs to leave Sunday afternoon and head back across the bridge to the *real world*, as Alice had come to think of life off the island. Like her life here was *unreal* in some way. Bekuh was Alice's Sunday-school friend since second grade. From youth choir and church camp to swim team and track meets, and later as bridesmaids and young mothers, they'd stayed in each other's lives. Bekuh was also an RN.

"You okay?" she asked, looking searchingly into Alice's eyes. "You seem tired."

"Champagne headache," Alice replied, "too many mimosas, that's all."

Alice touched her temples with her fingers, making small circles to chase away the beginnings of a throbbing pain behind her eyes. Her tongue felt sandpapery on the roof of her mouth. She bit it to keep herself from saying more. There was one secret she wasn't ready to spill yet, not even with her oldest friend.

"There's no such thing as too many mimosas," Bekuh said, with sparkling eyes. Bekuh had astigmatism that made her eyes twinkle in tandem, like merry metronomes. And with that, they laughed and hugged and promised to keep in touch.

It was only after her friends had headed back from the beach to the burbs—scattered to the "ettas" as they referred to the Atlanta-adjacent areas they called home—that Alice saw Skye again.

Sitting on the porch swing, Alice was sipping her nightly glass (or three) of white wine and watching the sun set over the ocean. She was feeling comfortably cozy, wrapped in a vanilla pashmina, savoring the juicy bits of gossip her friends had shared and replaying in her head some of the comical moments of the weekend. Like when she and her girls had been soaking— happily naked—in the hot tub of the fancy hotel spa thinking it was on the women's side of things, only to look up and see a Speedo-clad older gentleman shuffle into the apparently unisex steam room.

They watched in mute horror as he slipped off his Crocs and lowered himself slowly into their now-silent circle with a satisfied sigh. Alice and crew were holding their breath, not quite sure what to do, when he opened his eyes wide and beheld the bevy of blushing, bare-breasted women. A smile spread across his saggy jowls as he reached underwater and removed his swimsuit to wave it triumphantly overhead and then tossed it aside with a flourish.

"Let's party, ladies," he said, grinning from hair-tufted ear to ear.

Alice giggled at the memory as she watched the sun sink low through the cosmic layer cake of pinks, oranges and reds. She gently rocked herself back and forth with her freshly pedicured toes, a souvenir of the girls' weekend. Alice had chosen a bright blue for the polish. "Blue me away" it was called. Tabitha was making cashmere biscuits in her lap and purring happily, even drooling a little.

Alice had read somewhere that purring releases feel-good

endorphins and that cats use the low-frequency vibrations to soothe themselves. In fact, purring is a natural healing mechanism and may strengthen and repair bones, salve wounds and relieve pain. Alice wondered if she could teach herself how to purr like Tabitha.

Suddenly a little figure flitted across the sand. Alice stopped rocking and sat up abruptly. Perturbed, Tabitha jumped huffily to the floor. Then nothing. Silence except for the waves breaking on the beach.

There, behind the driftwood, Alice saw her again. Skye was wearing frayed denim Daisy Dukes and a tiny pale pink camisole. Alice could almost imagine the dainty silk rosebud on the front of the cami, although she couldn't see it from where she sat, stock still, peering into the quickly falling darkness. She also envisioned embroidery on the shorts. Perhaps a butterfly, but she could only see it in her mind. An image from childhood she couldn't quite place.

Just as her eyes focused on the silhouette of the small girl with the wild mane of hair, Alice saw Skye slip out of her clothes and tuck them inside a piece of driftwood. Then she flitted naked across the sand and flung herself headfirst into the ocean. Alice blinked hard and watched for Skye's head to pop up, her motherly instincts again on high alert. It was dark, and what about the undertow, and didn't sharks feed at night?

Alice stood up from the swing, her shawl slipping from her shoulders. And just as she was about to sprint across the beach and dive in after Skye, Alice saw a head and shoulders appear, much farther out than seemed safe or even possible. How could that waif of a girl have swum so far underwater? And then just as quickly she saw Skye's skinny arms reach overhead as she gracefully dipped back into the sea—and then Alice saw, well she *thought* she saw, a fish tail rise out of the water and splash back under. Like the whale tail from that insurance commercial only tinier, or perhaps more like the mermaid tail on a Starbucks cup.

CHAPTER 2

Finn took a last look around his soulless, spartan condo as he stuffed dirty clothes in his Tumi backpack. He unplugged the Keurig and checked the eyes on the stove to make sure they were off. Not that he had cooked anything since he'd been here. He lived on takeout and single-malt whisky. Hadn't bothered to hang a picture or otherwise personalize the Buckhead loft where he stayed when he had work to tend to in Atlanta. Finn had landed here after the divorce, well before really, when he and Sarah couldn't stand the sight of each other anymore.

They say women leave you emotionally before they ever leave you physically. That had definitely been the case with Sarah.

It wasn't that they didn't still love one another, but the abject pain reflected in each other's eyes was hard to bear. And yet, they couldn't look away. It was like having your own bottomless sorrow beamed back at you. After Lucy died, a piece of them died with her. And their marriage turned grey and drab. The light went out of their lives, and they were left with nothing but broken hearts that wouldn't heal.

They both blamed themselves and each other. Maybe it's like that when you lose a child. Your mind plays the events over and over on an endless loop, and you speculate about what you could have done. *If only I'd been paying attention. If only Sarah hadn't looked away. If only Lucy were less fearless and bold.*

But that was their Lucy, made of love dust and magic, their

late-in-life baby girl, who had instantly rocked their world. Distance runners, both of them, and high-powered attorneys, Finn and Sarah had no time for children. They were foodies and travelers, with an insatiable wanderlust that took them to remote villages and sparkling cities around the globe. They competed and won races. They savored indigenous dishes and immersed themselves in local culture. They climbed mountains and jumped out of helicopters to ski down glaciers in Switzerland. They had shamanic egg cleansings in Guatemala and took peyote in Mexico. Adrenaline junkies with no room for family beyond the two of them.

The Bermuda Half Marathon Derby had been a highlight of their travels. A picturesque run from one end of the island to the other, dating to 1909, the race is a beloved Bermuda Day tradition. Locals and tourists alike line the streets to cheer the runners on from St. George's to Hamilton and toast their quirky traditions with Rum Swizzles, Bermuda's national drink. The storied race takes place on the last Friday in May and is the first day Bermudians will go into the sea and also the first day Bermuda shorts are worn as business attire.

"You go to heaven if you want—I'd rather stay here in Bermuda," Mark Twain famously said.

Finn and Sarah ran the race and partied afterwards, ending up skinny-dipping at Horseshoe Bay long after most of the revelers had retired. Moonstruck and love-drunk, they slept on the beach, awakening on a bed of pink sand and shimmering sea glass. Because of the island's jagged coral reefs and shallow coastal waters, Bermuda has 500 years of shipwrecks beneath its waters. Remnants of whisky bottles, glass goblets and medicine vials worn smooth by the tides over the centuries wash up on the beaches like long-lost pirate's treasure.

Giddy and hungover, Finn and Sarah gathered sea glass as they scooped up their clothes and set off in search of the perfect fish sandwich with the works (deep-fried wahoo, lettuce, tomato, tartar sauce and coleslaw on toasted raisin bread). It was years later that Finn found their sea-glass stash in a Ziploc back in the back of a drawer—much to little Lucy's delight.

From then on, he'd walk along in front of her on the beach at Kennesaw, surreptitiously sprinkling sea glass for her to find. Little gems revealing themselves and winking in the sand. Lucy's giddy delight was Finn's greatest pleasure. Her childlike squeals, as she "discovered" the weathered, frosted glass, still wafted over the waves sometimes when he was running alone on the hard-packed sand.

The Isle of Skye Half Marathon had been the last race Finn and Sarah ran together before finding out they were pregnant with Lucy. Sarah was as fit and fierce as ever as they ran across the spongy green hills set against the craggy shoreline. After the race, they'd celebrated with prawn chowder and fish & chips at The Old Inn in Carbost, washed down with countless drams of Talisker. Finn smiled at the memory of playing darts with some locals while Sarah danced with a Shetland Islander on holiday. The guy was quite smitten with Sarah and had later found her on Facebook and tried to initiate a long-distance romance.

Finn and Sarah liked to think Lucy was conceived on the rugged, mystical island, home to the Faerie Glen and Castle Ewan where they pressed coins in the cracks of a small cave for good luck. Lucy was the happy surprise of their middle age. The child they didn't know they wanted. And she quickly become the epicenter of their universe.

Finn didn't understand why he kept the place on Kennesaw Island. It was so full of bittersweet memories. And yet he couldn't give it up. It wasn't that he was wallowing in his grief as much as he was holding on to the increasingly tenuous connection to Lucy, like a gossamer silk thread. He still saw her sometimes on the beach. Heard her sparkling peals of laughter erupt at unexpected moments, like when he was just waking up from a fitful sleep tangled in sweat-soaked sheets. Finn would bolt upright and dash into her empty room, heart pounding in his ears, hope draining from his heart.

He tended the garden Sarah and Lucy had planted with care. The heirloom tomatoes and Lucy's beloved watermelon vine. Sold the produce to The Beachcomber and to the island's one upscale restaurant, the Driftwood Kitchen. Farm-to-table all the way. They made delicious soups and sauces that tasted to Finn like lost love and heartache.

Finn was a masterful compartmentalizer. Able to suppress his feelings and immerse himself in the reams of paperwork his corporate law practice necessitated. Sarah had been the litigator. He was the calm, cool corporate attorney. He didn't compete in road races anymore, having lost his training partner. He didn't travel either. His passion for new experiences had burned out like a half-smoked cigarette forgotten in an ashtray. Finn still ran on the beach and scanned the waves for a bobbing blonde head. Sometimes he even saw one. He'd stop and blink and focus on the spot beyond where the surf breaks, but she'd be gone. In her place he'd see a pod of dolphins or a seagull gently riding the waves.

At the beach house, he kept Lucy's room just so. He knew this was not healthy or constructive or conducive to *moving on*. That's what his well-meaning friends and family were always encouraging him to do. *You've got to move on, Finn.* But he couldn't bring himself to pack up Lucy's things, her sweet-smelling little girl clothes and dolls and the stuffed unicorn that lived on the foot of her bed. He kept the door closed though. And only went in after several glasses of Talisker. Finn didn't allow himself to linger in his grief. He knew it was a luxury he couldn't afford. That if he fell too far into the abyss he'd lose his way back.

It had been nine years since Lucy drowned, although her little lifeless body had never been returned by the cold, callous ocean. Sarah had never recovered. Quit her law practice. Left their marriage. And disappeared. Sometimes he heard from mutual friends that she was traveling overseas or volunteering in some remote village. Teaching English or tending children. Once he even heard she'd remarried and had another child, but he found that hard to believe. How could she have *moved on* when he couldn't?

Sure, Finn dated. His colleagues in Atlanta were always keen to fix him up. And there was no shortage of attractive women on Kennesaw, particularly during the season. But Finn found it easier to skim the surface of relationships. Small talk. Fine wines. Boozy sex that didn't mean anything. He was careful not to commit. And that only seemed to make him more attractive to the women in his circle. Finn could never figure that out about women. Why they were drawn to men who weren't interested in them, who weren't interested in anything? Something about the female instinct to fix what was broken all to hell.

There was this new woman on the island, though. Alice. He'd run into her in the produce section at The Beachcomber and seen her at yoga a time or two. She was attractive and smart. In fact, her intelligence was palpable. Alice had whisky-brown hair with streaks of blonde and maybe grey? Could it be in the era of manicured, well-maintained women, Botoxed and bronzed, that Alice didn't color her hair? Her figure was nice and curvy in all the right places, but not perfectly sculpted like the llama-lashed hardbodies back at the Laughing Lotus. There was a softness to Alice that Finn found sexy. Her face was lived in and lined but still lovely.

It was her imperfection that made her, well, perfect, Finn thought.

Alice seemed as determined as he was to avoid romantic entanglements. At least that's the vibe he'd gotten from her. And he found that oddly appealing.

Back on the island in late November, Finn was running on the beach, the sand hard packed and the wind off the waves no gentle breeze. It was more like an icy slap in the face. The water was choppy, and the clouds hung so low it was hard to tell where the ocean ended and the sky began. He saw a figure up ahead, bundled in a poufy down jacket with a pom-pom-topped beanie pulled down over her ears. There was a scarf in between, wrapped around her neck and covering her face, burka like, so that only her eyes showed. Even obscured by her cocoon of clothing, she looked familiar somehow and, as he slowed to a walk, Finn recognized Alice.

She didn't notice him at first. Lost in thought, Alice gazed out at the sea as if she were searching for something. Then she shivered a little and rewrapped her woolen scarf around her neck. Cold. She was always cold now. Couldn't seem to get warm.

When she finally turned around, Finn was right in front of her. He hadn't meant to startle Alice, but she stumbled back and gave an audible gasp.

"Sorry, I didn't see you," Alice managed with a self-conscious laugh, after she collected herself. "Did you swim up out of the ocean or drop straight out of the sky?"

She was especially pretty when she smiled, Finn thought to himself. Her eyes squinted in the most adorable way. She had finely etched laugh lines that made her seem real. That was it. She didn't have the overly plumped, waxed, Instagram-filtered features that so many women favored these days—their curated appearances virtually interchangeable. It was like they were erasing their actual selves. Alice's face was unique and entirely her own.

"Didn't mean to scare you. There's not usually anyone on the beach this time of year," Finn answered, still marveling at all her layers. "You warm enough?"

Alice could tell he was teasing her. His eyes had that twinkle, and his head had that tilt to it. Maybe she was over bundled, but the wind was fierce. Finn, on the other hand, was clad only in running gear, water wicking, wind resistant, high tech and body hugging. She noted his lean physique and V-shaped torso. She took in his broad shoulders and trim waist, his perfectly shaped thighs and calves. Then she realized he was saying something. And she hadn't really been listening, so absorbed was she in his physical presence.

"So, there's only one restaurant still open in the off-season. The Driftwood Kitchen. Have you been there yet? Maybe we could have dinner this weekend if you're available? I've been in Atlanta for a while. I only just got back to the island, and I'd love the company."

So, it came to be that Alice and Finn had a date.

And after wine and candles, crème brûlée and convivial conversation, they ended up back at Alice's cottage. And although it had been a hot minute since either of them had slept with anyone, they did. And it was nice. They fit easily together, and it wasn't awkward or embarrassing or disappointing in any way. In fact, it was kind of magical. They rose and fell together like the ocean and the sky, like yoga and running, synchronizing breath and movement. And afterwards, they lay in each other's arms. Rather, she rested her head on his chest and folded herself into him, with his arm encompassing her, holding her steady. She felt safe. He felt the same way, for the first time in a long, long time.

Alice didn't think about her failed marriages and her most-recent angry ex. Finn didn't think about Sarah or the string of sexy strangers since. They drifted into a dreamless sleep, still gently clinging to each other. And as they shifted in their slumber, it became a somnambulate dance, their bodies moving in tandem until they fit together like tarnished silver spoons nestled in a felt-lined drawer.

In the morning, Tabitha walked over both of them, two bodies instead of the usual one. It didn't matter to her. She was hungry, and it was time for her human to feed her. Her feline routine was not to be interrupted.

Alice roused herself and padded to the kitchen, clad in her favorite ultra-mini UGG booties and a well-worn cashmere robe the color of charcoal, to feed the cat and make tea. She heard Finn in the shower. It felt good to have him here. She sighed a blissful sigh as she stared out the window over her steamy cup. She wondered absentmindedly if he could feel her tumors from the inside out. No, that was silly. Surely not.

And there had been no blood on the sheets. Alice had checked.

Then her eye caught a flash of movement among the driftwood. A disembodied blonde head bounced along just beyond the hulk of a particularly large piece of sea timber that looked like a prehistoric crocodile, inert but still dangerous. And there she was again, this time walking across the crocodile's spine, putting one bare foot in front of the other like a gymnast on a balance beam. The tiny sprite was clad improbably in a pink tutu with a matching fleece hoodie over it, but the hood had fallen down in the back, and Skye's irrepressible hair was dancing in the wind. The tutu looked like a cloud of cotton candy encircling Skye's slim hips. Alice noticed a pair of fluffy pink earmuffs completing the ensemble. It was the earmuffs that pierced her heart.

But those bare feet—she'll catch her death of cold, thought Alice, pulling herself out of her reverie and into action. She rapped on the glass with her knuckles even as she pulled off her UGGs knowing they'd be way too big for Skye, who had glanced up at Alice's worried face. The girl froze like a tiny pink deer. Alice motioned for her to come inside. Skye seemed to be considering it when another face appeared in the window.

Finn had come up behind Alice and wrapped his arms around her waist burying his nose in her neck. Pleasantly distracted, she dropped her boots and curled herself into his caress.

"Dreary day," Finn said after a moment, as he looked out at the sullen sea.

Alice glanced back up and saw that Skye had disappeared. She started to say something to Finn about the mysterious little girl but wasn't sure where to begin. And she didn't want him to think she was eccentric, or worse, crazy, because what if there wasn't really a little girl and she was all in Alice's head? The thought had crossed her mind more than once. She'd asked about Skye at yoga, and the yoginis had grown silent and exchanged knowing glances. It made Alice feel weird, so she'd stopped asking.

"Only one thing to do on a day like this," Finn said, kissing her ear and the top of her head.

"What's that?" Alice asked, twisting around to face him.

"Go back to bed," he said.

So, they did.

It was later in the week, after Finn had gone back to Atlanta, that Alice found herself at Evangeline's, the island's only bookstore, whose namesake and proprietress was an imposing woman. Evangeline had skin the color of dark chocolate. Her hair was a mass of beaded braids that she sometimes wrapped up in a pineapple topknot and sometimes wore down her back like an elegant ebony cape or a waterfall of writhing snakes.

Evangeline's grandmother had been a famous Gullah-Geechee storyteller and had passed on her passion for language to her granddaughter. Evangeline lovingly preserved the culture and traditions of her West African ancestors who settled on the Golden Isles of Georgia in the mid-1700s. Her shop featured woven seagrass baskets and tools, many of them museum quality and not for sale, as well as rare books and old photos documenting the Gullah Coast's tradition and heritage. Evangeline's was part museum, part bookstore, part gathering place, where islanders and tourists alike were drawn like dragonflies to warm flat stones.

You could rest at Evangeline's and gather your thoughts. Daydream and watch the dust motes dance in the sunbeams as they moved across the floor.

Alice loved to lose herself in Evangeline's collections of Geechee artifacts and asked endless questions about the history of this vanishing culture. Evangeline was always happy to expound on the legends and folklore of her people and how they came to be on Kennesaw Island. She was the keeper of the flame.

Evangeline also curated an extensive selection of books and materials devoted to the rehabilitation of sea turtles. Alice had learned that there are only seven species of sea turtles in the world and that five are found along Georgia's coast. Sea turtles return to the same beaches for nesting every year, migrating thousands of miles, from foraging grounds and back, throughout their lifetimes. Alice had become quite passionate about their preservation, as was Evangeline.

So, it was that the two women had bonded over books and their shared fervor for sea turtles and their reverence for those who came before them. Southerners are grounded by their sense of place, their respect for the land and their ancestors, cherished customs and past ways of life. Special foods that evoke memories. The oral tradition of storytelling. Music that makes you pine for something foreign yet familiar. These are the ties that bind. Whether your forebears hail from West Africa or the Hebrides off the northwest coast of Scotland, there's a kinship that comes from tending the generational fires.

Like sea turtles, Southerners always return to their homes, if not literally then figuratively. Where they were born and raised. Where they come from. It defines them and shapes them forever. Their worldview is always colored by the lens of their childhood.

Evangeline had papered her bookstore with memories over the years, commemorating events large and small in the life of Kennesaw Island. It was a kaleidoscope of postcards and Polaroids, newspaper clippings and sepia-toned black and white photos. As Alice sipped her peppermint tea and chatted with Evangeline, she glanced at the collage of old photos and new ones that lined the walls behind the comfy cognac leather reading chairs.

Suddenly a particular snapshot caught Alice's eye.

She recognized immediately a younger version of Finn with a beautiful blue-eyed brunette. They were laughing and smiling in the picture. Alice was mesmerized by the woman's other-worldly blue eyes, her ocean eyes. So much so that it took her a moment to notice the adorable toddler between Finn and his wife. A chubby-cheeked cherub with an orb of white-blonde curls around her head. She looked like a dandelion. And she was smiling so big, her eyes were completely shut in a deliriously happy squint. In her hands she clutched a melting ice cream cone, the vanilla dripping down her pudgy fingers all the way to her adorably dimpled wrists. Sweet milky rivulets against her downy, golden skin.

"That picture, that little girl," Alice blurted out, interrupting Evangeline in mid-sentence. "With Finn. At least I think that's Finn," she added, trying not to sound too interested.

Alice wasn't sure what to make of her budding romance, if you could call it that. Or if she wanted to share it with her new friend. So far it was just a few flirty encounters, an intimate dinner and a wonderful lost weekend. Alice didn't know how she felt about Finn, or what they had together, if anything.

"Which one are you looking at?"

Evangeline swiveled in her seat to gaze over the rims of her turquoise tortoise-shell readers at the wall behind her. Alice pointed to the picture held in place with a pink thumbtack.

"Oh, that's Lucy, such a sweet little thing; Sarah and Finn's baby girl."

Evangeline was shaking her head now from side to side, and her tone had grown somber.

"So sad. So sad," she said softly, as she turned back to face Alice.

Alice stared wide-eyed and silent at Evangeline, willing her to go on.

"You know that little girl could swim like a fish. It was such a tragedy. Such a tragedy," said Evangeline, taking a sip of her hibiscus tea and staring off into space, clearly lost in thought.

"What happened?" asked Alice after a minute or two had passed with no further comment from Evangeline. She was almost afraid to find out.

"She drowned is what happened," Evangeline said with a deep sigh. "You know how it goes. It's every mother's nightmare. You try to be ever-vigilant, always watching. It was a few years after that picture was taken. Lucy just disappeared into the blue waves in the blink of an eye."

Alice held her breath, and Evangeline began to tell the story Alice had been waiting to hear.

"It was late summer, and there was a red tide," explained Evangeline, her eyes closed now, and she conjured up the painful memory. "That's when the ocean blooms with dinoflagellates, tiny phytoplankton that blanket the water, turning it the color of dried blood by day. At night, it's an iridescent blue. Bioluminescence, it's called." Evangeline enunciated the strange word, so it sounded almost lyrical as it rolled off her lips.

"Anyhow, this phenomenon creates a neon wave that's best viewed after dark. The commotion of the waves beating against the shore disturbs the little creatures—which are neither plant nor animal—and causes them to emit light, like millions of underwater fireflies.

"Finn and Sarah were on the beach with everyone else, bearing witness to nature's miracle. It was pitch black that night. I don't know where the stars went or why they left us. The moon was hiding, too, but that only made the ocean seem to shine even brighter. We all stared at the water, transfixed by the luminous waves. It was one of those moments, like a lunar eclipse or fireworks display that's best witnessed in silence, punctuated with lots of ooohs and ahhs."

Evangeline took a sip of her tea and closed her eyes. Alice thought of the Blue Grotto, the sea cave she'd visited once on the coast of Capri in Southern Italy, where sunlight shines through seawater eerily illuminating the cavern. It had been hypnotizing.

"I think we were all lulled into complacence by the ocean that night. Bioluminescence comes from a chemical called luciferase, same root as 'Lucifer' which literally means 'light bearer.'"

Alice closed her eyes now too, to see the story Evangeline was telling.

"Lucy was darting around like a little hummingbird. She was up past her bedtime, hyper and delirious with that special adrenaline that only children can feel in the presence of something magical. She and a flock of younglings were running around in circles and making sand angels. Acting wild but feeling safe within the orbit of their parents. You know that sense of danger that's just enough to give you goosebumps, but you can still see your folks out of the corner of your eyes, so you know you're okay?

"Well, the grown-ups got to talking and lost track of the little ones. The children sensed it, a loosening of the parental grip, and they were drunk on it. Giddy and giggling. Clamoring over rocks and playing hide and seek behind the driftwood. You could hear their manic laughter rising above the sound of the breaking waves.

"Folks had their eyes on the ocean and their ears on their little ones. Put me in mind of how penguins can recognize the call of their babies. They can hear them even when they can't see them. Can pick their chicks out of a colony of squawking, tuxedo-clad birds. It's a species-survival thing—so they only feed their own fledglings. A phenomenon known as the 'cocktail party effect.'"

Evangeline was shaking her head from side to side in amazement. She gave a rueful laugh as her eyes filled with unshed tears.

"I remember seeing Lucy chasing the tide in and out, dancing in the surf like a sea sparrow.

"When it came time to gather up the children and head home, families packed up their coolers and shook out their towels. Folded up their chairs and scooped up their sleepy-headed little ones. It was the calm before the storm.

"I heard Sarah calling for Lucy. Calmly at first, but with a mother's urgency. Then her cries turned frantic. Finn was looking everywhere and hollering Lucy's name, too. We all joined in, those of us that remained. Some folks went home and got flashlights and came back to comb the beach, but no Lucy. The other children were shaken awake and gently interrogated. They all remembered Lucy wading out in the water. Every single one of them heard the siren's call of their fearless playmate. She had encouraged them to join her, but they were afraid of the spooky blue water with the lightning bolts in it. Not Lucy, though. She was bold and brave. And like I said, she could swim like a fish.

"Then the authorities got involved. Coast Guard boats churned those neon waves that night and then day and night for the next week. We organized search parties and prayer vigils and kept watch, scanning the sea till our eyes blurred. Fishermen took out their own skiffs after the Coast Guard quit looking. We're close knit here on the island. I don't think Finn slept the whole time. When they finally called off the search, Sarah collapsed into herself and took to her bed. Everything came apart after that. How does a mother grieve for her child when she can't even hold her little limp body in her arms?"

Evangeline was standing now, lost in thought in front of the old photo, as silent tears streamed down her face. She had put her cup down and had one hand on her heart. With her other hand, she reached out and placed her finger gently just below Lucy's face.

"Sarah loved that little girl something fierce. She never got over it. Neither did Finn."

Standing behind Evangeline now, Alice was still in shock as she stared at the picture. Her heart was racing, and her mind was jumbled with a million thoughts at once. She tried to make sense out of what she was seeing and hearing. Because the smiling little girl in the photo surrounded by her adoring parents was a younger version of someone Alice knew.

It was Skye.

33

CHAPTER 3

She didn't remember, that was the thing. She just didn't remember. Who the man was who ran on the beach, whose house she sometimes snuck into. She knew he was someone very dear to her. Very important in her life. When she opened the bedroom window, she wondered if he left it unlocked on purpose just for her. She'd sit on the silky quilted bedspread under the lace canopy and pat the stuffed unicorn. She felt at home here, but she also felt restless. Like she didn't quite belong. She'd open the drawers of the little white dresser and see the neatly folded clothes scented with homemade rosemary sachets. She took only what she needed, which wasn't much. She could wear something over and over for ages until it fell apart. But sometimes when she tucked her clothes into driftwood crevices or between the rocks at the beach, they weren't there when she came back. Washed away or carefully removed by some well-intentioned beachcomber tidying up.

She looked at the pictures on the bedside table. Saw the smiling beautiful woman and the running man. They felt familiar and unfamiliar at the same time. Like a memory swimming in the back of your brain that just won't surface.

She ran her hands through the silky sea glass in the jewelry box with the little ballerina on it. The box played music when you opened it, and the dancer twirled slowly in a stiff pirouette. The sea glass shone like diamonds in the moonlight as it reflected off the ocean and poured through the windows.

Skye's life now was the ocean. The endless green sea. She swam and swam and never got tired, never had to come up for air. The water was a second skin for her. The silence was a gift. And the other creatures that lived there accepted her and left her alone. Once she was submerged, she was safe. That's all she knew. She was safe in this watery womb. She was home.

Curiosity drove her to climb out of the waves and walk on dry land sometimes. It felt weird at first and took some getting used to. But then it was like she belonged there, too. She loved the feel of the gritty, wet sand and the dry, dusty driftwood. But mostly it was the sun she craved. That first breath she took when she broke the surface after swimming toward the light. It was dazzling. Her lungs filled with air, and the sunlight hit her in the face like the blinding smile of the universe. Sometimes she'd lie there on the rocks just soaking up the sun, baking her body with its warmth. As her skin dried, her scales fell away leaving long lithe limbs where her shimmering tail had been.

She didn't question it. It was all she had ever known. All she could remember. This duality. This life above and below the sea. A leopard doesn't wonder about its spots.

There's a school of thought called the Aquatic Ape Theory that suggests our ancestors spent a significant portion of their lives in the sea. More amphibious mammals than terrestrial hominids, these mostly hairless humans foraged underwater for aquatic food—sea spinach, edible tubers, and later shellfish. According to this theory, our forebears eventually returned to land over many millennia to became bipedal omnivores and then hunters. In fact, coastal tribes still practice a bimodal diving pattern, like sea otters, to scavenge for food, precious shells and pearls.

Humans are the best swimmers and divers among the apes. Our straight, streamlined bodies and smooth skin surface reduce drag. We have flexible backbones that allow us to perform the lift-based "dolphin kick" while submerged. We can equalize our ears at depth. As infants, we have an innate diving reflex whereby we open our eyes and hold our breath underwater and propel ourselves forward with rhythmic limb movements. Babies are instinctually able to swim and dive before being able to crawl and walk. They have no fear of immersion.

But Skye didn't know any of this. She only knew that the ocean was her world.

And now there was this woman. This other woman. Skye felt a connection to her, the kind lady in the little cottage with the porch swing and the clattering windchimes and the fluffy kitty cat. There had been another someone, another woman in her life. She was sure of it, at least sometimes. The lady in the pictures with the running man. Other times, she thought maybe it was just a dream. Of a time before now. A life before this one.

She saw the running man once in the window with the cat lady, and they looked happy. And that made her little selkie soul smile. But she also knew Alice—that was the woman's name, because she had told her—she knew that Alice had a secret she hadn't told the running man. Or anyone else. Something she kept to herself, and it was eating her up inside.

You see, Alice was sick.

CHAPTER 4

Sinking into the water, Alice watched steam rise and swirl around her. She was aware of the black and white tile floor; the shaggy looped bathmat and the damask cotton towels she had bleached and folded while they were still warm. She had smudged the bathroom with sage before she got in the tub and opened the window to hear the sea and watch the beach grass sway in the breeze. She added lavender bath salts to the running water, feeling the crystals fall between her fingers.

Alice was a creature of water. Always had been.

She parked her wet soapy feet on the edge of the porcelain and spread her toes, imagining webbing between them. In fact, when she put her heels together and closed her eyes a little, her feet fanned out like a fish tail. There was a teak tray across the center of the tub that slid back and forth. Alice had scooted it just past the midway point so she could reach her wine glass, her loofah sponge, and her island-made thyme soap from Evangeline's.

The hot water took the edge off the pain she felt low in her belly and her back. She glanced at the medicine cabinet, fogged up now from the bathwater. Alice knew it held a vial of morphine for when her bones ached from the inside out. It was a last resort. For now, she used cannabis oil and gummies, meditation and breathing exercises. And wine, lots of wine.

Alice had always felt most at home in water. From an early

age, the big deep bathtub in her family's 1920s-era bathroom had been a sanctuary. As a child, Alice loved that the bathroom had never been updated. Its cool marble walls contained generations of secrets, like a tomb. She was just part of a long line of souls to share this space. Because she was an empath, Alice felt all this in her bones as she soaked in the tub, without knowing that other people didn't experience life in quite the same way.

Even though she shared the bathroom with her siblings, Alice could lock the door and fill the old ceramic basin with scalding water. There was a rubber cork on a beaded metal chain to block the drain. Alice loved the satisfying *glub-glub* sound of the tight seal finding its place. She'd float for ages, adding more hot water till it ran out and then soaking washcloths in the tepid water and draping them across her chest to stay warm. She'd hold her breath and submerge herself, feeling safe and serene, surrounded by the magnified sounds of her limbs knocking into the sides of the tub or of bubbles leaking from her nose between her tightly pinched fingers.

Sensory deprivation tanks and flotation therapy weren't widely embraced when Alice was a child. At least not in suburban Georgia. But even as a little girl, Alice intuitively felt the healing power of water and its all-encompassing embrace. Like the most wonderful hug from someone who loves you to the moon and back and never lets go. She didn't know it then, but Alice would search for that perfect hug her whole life.

From bathtubs to backyard pools to the lakes of Central Georgia, Alice's aquatic experiences were mostly landlocked until the summer after fourth grade. That's when her family made their first pilgrimage to Fort Lauderdale, with Alice and her siblings tightly packed like three sardines in the backseat of the unair-conditioned car. Windows rolled all the way down, with cranking levers, you could flap your arms like a seagull riding the stiff beach breeze. And the salty smell was unfiltered by ventilation. It smacked you right in the face and swept up your nose like a tidal wave.

Sometimes her sister got to ride up front with her parents because she got queasy. That's when Alice and her brother would climb into the back window and watch the sky and the clouds whoosh by until they spotted the first palm trees. This was before the time of seatbelts and car seats, so the intoxicating backwards view was entirely accessible.

Nothing was artificially rendered or photoshopped back then. It was authentic and real, and everyone felt alive and in the moment. Not like zombies swiping through life on a screen. What a golden era to grow up in.

On these interminable road trips, Alice's family would stop along the way for fresh-squeezed orange juice at roadside stands, occasionally spending the night at a Howard Johnson's and swimming in the motel pool, another delightful experience. Diving for pennies and walking tippy-toed along the rough pool surface until her feet bled, Alice would emerge, red-eyed and chlorinated, only to eat hamburgers and ice cream at the adjoining restaurant, another thrill.

The achingly cold vanilla scoop was served in a pewter pedestal dish on a scallop-edged paper coaster. Despite the inevitable brain freeze, it tasted way better than plain old ice cream from a carton at home. Alice thought this was the height of sophistication, as she sat shivering from sunburn in the overly air-conditioned dining room of the motor lodge.

Arriving at the actual beach and running down the sand into the bracing surf was beyond thrilling. Alice, her brother and her sister, sometimes joined by their dad, if he was feeling exuberant, would bob and float for what seemed like hours, letting the waves lift them and lower them in an unpredictable cadence that was irresistible. Alice would lie on her back, not even caring that the ocean was spilling into her ears. She'd stay like that as long as she could until she got too scared the next big wave would crash over her head or until it actually did.

There were techniques they developed, the three of them back in the '70s, before goggles and water wings, before sun-protective gear and shoes you wore in the surf. It was just you versus the ocean,

Mother Nature at her most seductive. You had to be vigilant and pay attention to everything around you.

Sometimes when a giant wave was about to break, Alice would dive underneath it and hear its crash and boom overhead, hoping she could hold her breath until it passed. She'd hover there in stasis, cheeks puffed out, eyes wide open in the murky churning water, like a lost soul, suspended in time and space. Alice felt forgotten by her laughing family, bobbing on the surface above her head. It was as though she had a secret life beneath the waves.

Alice and her sibs would eventually stumble back to the beach house across the road from the actual beach, sunburnt and salty, sand in every crevice of their bodies, eyes puffy and hair tangled, hearts full. Food tasted better after a day in the ocean. Sleep came fast in cool sheets with Noxema on noses and damp squeaky hair on cool cotton pillowcases.

Now, a lifetime later, Alice was back at the beach, on Kennesaw Island, not Florida's southeastern coast. But the feeling was the same. The ocean was her haven, and those family beach trips were her most cherished childhood memory.

Alice was soaking in the tub with a glass of wine in her hand and Tabitha purring on the bathmat beside her. She thought back to that fateful visit to her gynecologist. It still seemed surreal.

It had been a few years since Alice had been to the doctor. It didn't seem important. She was rarely sick and had no chronic conditions. Her blood pressure ran low. She took no medications other than a multi-vitamin and a Tums for calcium. She was past her child-bearing years and had already surfed the tumultuous waves of menopause without hormone treatments. Scott was in basic training. Work was crazy hectic.

After several cancellations and postponements, Alice finally made time for a long-overdue well visit. Even then, it was more about the mammogram than the pap smear. There was so much peer pressure around breast cancer. She had friends of friends and acquaintances who'd suffered from the disease. She'd heard tell of their bodies ravaged and disfigured. Their hair fell out from the treatments. Then there were the complications. Always complications. Metastasis and insidious infections. Heart damage, neuropathy, and lingering pain, which sometimes seemed worse than the illness itself.

Some of them made it through, and some of them didn't. It was a sobering sad reality of Alice's age group. And the ones that didn't make it were lauded for their brave fights. Everyone always talked about *fighting* breast cancer or *surviving* it, like you were at war with your own body. There were GoFundMe pages devoted to it.

But nobody talked about cervical cancer. There were no self-exams and buddy checks for that. No pink ribbons, 5Ks or fundraising galas. In fact, cervical cancer shares a ribbon color with ovarian cancer: teal. It doesn't even rate its own ribbon. Somehow, breast cancer sucks all the air out of the room in the cancer conversation.

Alice recalled the sudden pain of the cold, metal speculum—creaking and clicking like a medieval torture device—and the sharp twinge of the spatula scraping live tissue from inside her sacred female space. She winced at the memory of it.

The pelvic exam is a physical and energetic violation universally dreaded by women everywhere. No matter how many times you go through it, there's no "normalizing" the experience. Incidentally, the speculum was devised by male gynecologists in the 19th century and has changed little since then.

When Alice's doctor told her she needed to have additional tissue removed and biopsied, she procrastinated. She scheduled the appointment and ended up canceling and rescheduling several times due to work conflicts and a natural aversion to the whole business, which triggered generational trauma from deep in her pelvic bowl.

Then she went to Scott's graduation from basic training in Austin and scheduled a visit to California while he was in tech school. There was work travel and a trip to New Orleans with a foodie friend. Also, a yoga retreat in Costa Rica, where the moon kissed the ocean and heart-shaped shells and stones appeared on the shore at sunrise. Life was full of surprises.

Alice felt fine. And maybe, on some level, she didn't want

anyone to tell her she wasn't fine. Weeks went by, then months. The doctor's office called and sent letters. She ignored them.

By the time she got around to it, the simple procedure revealed abnormal cervical lesions, which led to more tests and then a dismal diagnosis. Stage 4B cancer. In her liver and lymph nodes. Spots on her lungs and her spine. It was inconceivable that all this had snuck up on her with virtually no symptoms whatsoever.

Oh, there were options, aggressive treatments to attack her aggressive tumors. A radical hysterectomy was suggested, even though her cancer had already breached the boundaries of her cervix and uterus. The doctors wanted to carve out her feminine core as an afterthought. Alice declined.

She had watched both of her parents succumb to the complications of cancer. She'd heard countless stories of people battling the disease and extending their lives for a few months or even years. Some were even cancer free for long periods of time. But cancer became a shadowy figure that dogged them for the rest of their days.

The C-word. An unspeakable menace. Once it got its fangs in you, it never really let go. Your life was forever changed, and you were no longer in charge. Not that you ever were, but the false bravado of the illusion of control was shattered forever.

A dear friend in Alice's adult-curated inner circle (not her OG crew from childhood) had survived uterine cancer. She had a devoted husband and plenty of money and didn't work. It had been grueling, but she had persevered and kept a positive attitude throughout the ordeal. She had a collection of wigs made of real hair and dyed to match her own. Hired a trauma yoga instructor to give her private sessions in her home studio. Ate nourishing meals brought by attentive friends. And leaned on her ever-vigilant husband, who had his own contracting business, working remotely, between fly-fishing trips to their second home in Montana.

She was loved and cared for tenderly for the duration of her treatment. And when she rang the bell at the chemo center, the angels sang, because this woman was a saint and would go on to minister to others. Now she was savoring every precious moment with her children and grandbabies, keeping her family close as she kept constant vigil for the silent killer's return.

Alice was a realist. She was nothing if not pragmatic. How could she work and undergo chemo treatments? Who would care for her and make her soup and shop for wigs? How would she afford the out-of-pocket expenses and the Proton Therapy, that wasn't covered by insurance? The cold hard reality was that Alice couldn't afford to fight her cancer. She didn't want to derail Scott's life. And she didn't have anyone else to turn to. A sister in Memphis. A brother in Miami. But they had their own problems and jobs and spouses and children. No one had time to drop everything and put their lives on hold for Alice. Just as her parents hadn't wanted to be a burden, physically, emotionally or financially, Alice didn't either. Caring for them had been rewarding but exhausting. She wouldn't wish it on anyone, least of all her only child.

The beach, any beach, was her spiritual home, and it had been calling her back for some time now. Instinctually, Alice knew where she wanted to end her days. She didn't want to fight. She wanted to embrace her destiny and see it through to its logical conclusion. With as much grace as she could muster.

She thought about Tabitha and made a mental note to ask Evangeline to look after her when she was gone. Alice still had not told her newest friend about her health, or her unhealth, as it were. She wanted to keep the magic going a little bit longer. This happy, simple life she'd built for herself here on Kennesaw. The soothing routine of it. Evangeline, Finn, what about Finn? She didn't know. And Skye, if she even existed and was not, in fact a Fig Newton of Alice's increasingly vivid imagination. Maybe Skye was a hallucination. Didn't Alice sometimes see her wearing clothes she herself had worn as a child? That navy blue monogrammed one-piece bathing suit from her camp days? It didn't make any sense.

Sometimes, Alice felt woolly headed and foggy brained. Was it the cancer or the remedies to keep it at bay that caused her befuddlement?

Alice absentmindedly added more hot water to her bath, turning the faucet with her prehensile toes. She thought about the cat she'd had before Tabitha. He was an orange tiger cat, named David. He was independent and dignified. When he died, it had happened quickly. Alice hadn't even realized he was sick. Animals hide their frailties so as not to appear weak and vulnerable to predators. But Alice preferred to think of it as the quiet, cat-like dignity that defined David's existence. Of course, she noticed his waning appetite and his increasingly unkempt coat, but she had chalked it up to old age. When Dr. Bea, the visiting vet, paid a house call and confirmed the cancerous tumors in David's belly, there was nothing that could be done. He died a week later, in the neighbor's driveway near the trashcans. Cats usually go away to die discreetly, on their own terms.

Alice had known when the neighbor knocked on her door as she was getting ready for work that fateful morning. She had followed him across the wet lawn, still clad in her bathrobe and crying copiously, to scoop up her beloved companion, wet from the rain, rigor mortis already setting in. She had recently ordered a biodegradable pet pod to bury him in when the time came.

Even during her grief, Alice marveled at David's thoughtfulness, going far enough away to die privately, but not so far away that he couldn't be found, leaving Alice forlorn, forever wondering.

She tried to go to work but was overcome with emotion and sent home by her kindly boss. Her work buddies showed up at the house unannounced, bearing wine and keeping Alice company as she blow-dried her dead cat with her hair dryer and tenderly picked the dirt from his pink-padded paws. Scott had still been in high school at the time. When he got home after soccer practice, he'd dug the hole in the flower bed, among the Lenten Roses, where David was laid to rest.

Alice had been broken up about it but had always admired David's restraint. It was a precursor to her parents' later deaths, also of cancer, exacerbated by old age. And to their astonishing grace in the face of all the unpleasantness their illnesses entailed. They never flinched, her parents. Not once. They were her role models. This was how it was done. None of the flailing about and hand wringing, no long-drawn-out treatments, where the quixotic cure is worse than the malady itself. Her parents had seen too many of their peers made miserable in the last years of their lives by wishful thinking and opportunistic doctors. Alice's folks had accepted their fates and met death with quiet dignity. Like David, the cat.

And so, when Alice heard her own dire prognosis, she calmly accepted her fate. She decided to let nature take its course. Her doctor said she had six months, maybe a year. That's when she'd sold everything and put her affairs in order, updated her will and her healthcare directives. She told no one about her condition. Named an attorney as executor in the event of her death. Made sure Scott was named as beneficiary on all the paperwork.

There was still a small storage space full of cardboard boxes with lids, the kind that reams of typing paper come in. One for every year of Scott's childhood. Hastily marked with Sharpies. *Scott Kindergarten. Scott Second Grade. Scott Senior Year.*

Where had the time gone? Alice had been a harried single mom, working full time and raising her son all by herself. T-ball, soccer, swim team, chess club, sleepovers, birthday parties and braces. Driving lessons, prom, high school graduation. Moving him into the dorm at her alma mater, the University of Georgia. *Go Dawgs! Sic 'em! Woof! Woof! Woof! Woof! Woof!*

And finally, she'd seen Scott off to basic training, with the other proud, patriotic parents, who took Alice under their wings, as she stood alone waving goodbye to her only son.

She'd always meant to go back to those boxes, stuffed with drawings and snapshots and favorite toys long forgotten. They were precious time capsules, chronicling both Scott's childhood and Alice's motherhood. She had meant to make scrapbooks or maybe a montage video set to music to play at Scott's rehearsal dinner when he finally met and married his soulmate, whom he'd yet to find.

Those boxes were her final link to the best part of her life. Being a mother. She'd embraced the role and loved every single damn minute of it. Some people achieve great things in life. The way Alice looked at it, her purpose on Earth had been to give birth to and raise her wonderful, magical, brilliant, beautiful son. Her Indigo Child. And she had fulfilled that purpose.

Her only undone thing, the only item on her color-coded Post-It Notes she didn't get to cross off, was to open and sort through those boxes. Alice just couldn't do it. It would make dying too hard. She'd have second thoughts about not seeking treatment. She'd wonder and hope and go down the rabbit hole of what ifs and maybes.

Instead, she's rented a small, climate-controlled storage space and lovingly placed each box there. In order. Then she'd given the key to her lawyer to give to Scott. It was her thank you note to her child for being born and for the privilege of being his mother, which was her greatest joy in life.

Then she'd packed up her cat and headed to Kennesaw Island and the cozy cottage on Sea Star Lane. The Mermaid Cottage, as she'd come to think of it.

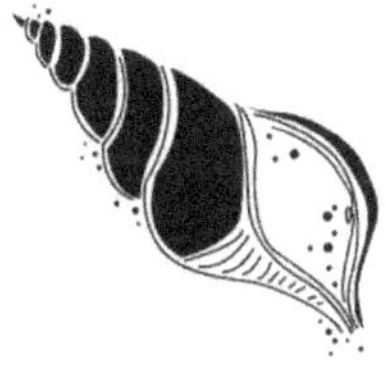

CHAPTER 5

Evangeline had grown up on Kennesaw Island, raised by her grand-mother, aka Grannie Annie, whose full name was Anyika Mariama Sullivan. Grannie Annie lived in two worlds. She easily traveled back and forth between the present and the past. She made fish stew from scratch and loved fast food in Styrofoam boxes. She practiced Gullah traditions and was also a God-fearing Evangelical Protestant, making sure Evangeline showed up at church every week in her Sunday best, including a stiff, starched petticoat under her dress and shiny black Mary Janes on her feet. Her lace-trimmed white cotton ankle socks were turned down just so.

Grannie Annie wanted to cover her bases where her precious granddaughter was concerned. Evangeline was "dipped" by the preacher as well as immersed in Gullah folk practices and beliefs. Evangeline soaked up the culture, especially the music and the distinctive spiritual rituals—the Lowcountry claps and ecstatic ring shouts. Grannie Annie regularly conversed with the dead, mostly her ancestors, and she taught Evangeline to do the same.

This was unusual in the 1970s when Evangeline just wanted to listen to Top 40 music on the radio, blow Hubba Bubba bubbles and wear blue eyeshadow like her friends. She lived in two worlds, too, but not as comfortably as her grandmother. Evangeline was constantly conflicted and confused. Part of her was firmly planted in her heritage, but another part of her couldn't wait to grow up and leave her peculiar childhood behind.

Evangeline left Kennesaw Island to escape her upbringing in college but ended up majoring in African Studies at Georgia Southern. By that time Grannie Annie, who had always been old—and was possibly Evangeline's great grandmother rather than her grandmother—was feeble and frail. Instead of the past, she traveled between this world and the next, so that Evangeline was never sure if she was fully present in either when she came home from school to visit.

As many of us do, when she left her hometown, Evangeline came to appreciate it more and more. It's the ultimate paradox. You have to move away to love where you came from. It's the distance that offers fresh perspective. You come to terms with what shaped you and then accept that sense of place in your heart. Evangeline returned to Kennesaw, ultimately settling there after a stint in the Peace Corps. She was in Sierra Leone when her beloved grandmother left this world for good.

Heartbroken, Evangeline came back months later to an empty house. Grannie Annie's bed was neatly made, and her slippers were still tucked underneath it. Evangeline opened the windows to let the sea air in, as the lace curtains danced on the breeze. She thought she heard the Gullah-Geechee call-and-response led by Grannie Annie wafting in the gentle wind.

Songs were given to us at birth. We will sing them for all we are worth, her grandmother was fond of saying. *You have to know where you came from to know where you're going.*

And that was when Evangeline knew she would stay on the island and dedicate her life to preserving the fragile culture of her people.

It was early March, and the island was coming to life again, showing signs of spring. The season's first tourists were browsing happily through the bookstore. Evangeline loved the little tinkling sound of the door chimes every time a visitor walked in. Her head snapped up in a Pavlovian way as she smiled and wondered what this or that person's story was. Evangeline was able to collect people's stories, just like her grandmother before her, because she listened with her heart.

Sometimes she greeted old friends, returning year after year to Kennesaw, here now to stock up on books to read on the beach or in softly swaying hammocks. Sometimes there were new faces, looking uncertain yet hopeful as their eyes adjusted to the warm glow of Evangeline's store and the welcoming presence of the charismatic woman herself.

Evangeline thought of the first time Alice had poked her head in the shop, with a cheery hello that sounded more like a song than a salutation. Their connection was instant. She and Alice had become fast friends. So, when Alice called and breathlessly described the "mermaid under the porch" she had discovered, Evangeline put the "Gone Fishin'" sign on the door of her shop and headed over to see for herself.

As she pulled into the little gravel driveway in her battered Jeep, she could hear a commotion out back. She walked through the open front door straight through the house and out onto the back porch, where Tabitha was swishing her tail and peering over the edge. Evangeline sat down beside the old cat and stroked her back as she listened to Alice grunt and grumble beneath the porch.

"What are you into now, woman?" she shouted above the roar of the ocean.

"Come and see!" was all Alice would say.

When Evangeline leaned over to peek through the lattice-work, she saw a mermaid staring back at her with wild yellow hair, ruby lips, and enormous bare breasts, although the breasts were somewhat cracked and faded. The semi-naked siren was a carved wooden figurehead from the bow of a ship. And for some reason, she'd been slumbering under Alice's cottage.

"Don't just stand there, get under here and help me get her out," squealed Alice.

Together they dragged the figurehead out into the sunlight. She was surprisingly heavy. They brushed the sand off and examined their treasure. She was made of oak, with intricate carved scales in various shades of green and blue covering her generous hips and thighs ending in an upturned fishtail. Her golden tresses traced the outline of her aforementioned massive breasts and followed her form with delicate curls down to her waist. She bore more than a striking resemblance to Dolly Parton. Perhaps she was an Appalachian mermaid. The two women struggled to right her as Dolly insisted on listing to one side.

"We need help," said Evangeline as she, Alice and the mermaid all collapsed in the sand together.

When Finn arrived, Alice and Evangeline were sipping margaritas in the shade on the porch swing, bare feet dangling, giggles rising with the tide. The figurehead was still resting on her side in the sun, like a garish tourist who'd fallen asleep on the beach.

"Ahoy, matey," called Alice. "We abandoned ship!"

More laughter ensued. The margaritas made everything funnier.

"Well, well, what have we here," muttered Finn, rubbing his incredibly sexy stubbly chin with the back of his hand, at least that's how it looked to Alice, who was bringing him a chilled beer.

"Finn, meet Dolly," said Alice, making the introductions to the supine siren.

"The pleasure's all mine, Dolly," Finn replied with a slight bow, as he eyed her ample bosom.

Then Finn took a long swig of his beer and met Alice's playful eyes. He broke the mutual stare with a wink and headed back to his truck to rummage around for tools and supplies.

Hours later—but it felt like days—Finn, Alice, Evangeline, and Tabitha sat on the porch steps gazing at their masterpiece. Dolly the Mermaid was upright and facing the sea, mounted on her own pedestal of driftwood and rocks, held together discreetly with wire and mortar. There had been some debate about using the driftwood from the beach. Was it protected like dune grass? Was there some law against moving it? But in the end, Finn, being an attorney, decided that the driftwood wasn't technically removed from the beach, and they were merely repurposing it to support another artifact the sea had offered up. Evangeline and Alice had threaded shells, sargassum and wooden beads along the wire so the figurehead's base was festive and beachy, befitting of the battered but beautiful siren of the sea.

Margaritas and beer had given way to tequila shots. Evangeline snored softly on the sofa, covered in quilts and a feline blanket, purring like a freight train, happily making biscuits on her back.

As for Alice and Finn, they stayed in the porch swing long into the night, rocking and talking, learning each other's lives. Alice waxed rhapsodic speaking of Scott, the apple of her eye. She glossed over her exes and talked instead about yoga and what a profound difference it had made and still did in her life. Finn spoke of his failed marriage and of Lucy. The story slipped out with starts and stops. Silence broken by bits and pieces, like the fragments of shells that dotted the moonlit beach.

Alice glanced out at the ocean, now smooth as glass, reflecting the stars back at themselves. She couldn't bring herself to mention Skye. It seemed cruel and at the same time overly fanciful. She didn't know who or what the little mermaid was, but she knew in her aching bones that Skye was a secret to be kept, like the deteriorating state of Alice's own health.

The next morning after her friends left, Alice walked down to the beach and gazed out at the ocean. She was comforted by its constancy. The waves breaking rhythmically like the heartbeat of the Earth. The whisper of the surf as it made its way up the shore sounded like the fizzing of a just-poured ginger ale. Often, her footprints were the first on the sand in the morning. It felt like a secret, a special privilege, perhaps a private pact between Alice and the sea. The day fresh and full of promise. Literally anything could happen. And she felt hopeful, despite the dull ache in her lower back and the intermittent pangs in her abdomen, so reminiscent of labor pains but different.

She watched a father and his tiny tot run to and from the water and was reminded of Scott when he was small. How well she remembered his first beach trip and how fearless he was in the face of the waves. He perched on Alice's hip as she waded in deeper and deeper, one thumb in his mouth, the other clutching a fistful of her hair. Scott was so trusting, so certain that he was safe in her arms. And he was. Despite his father's palpable discomfort back on shore. Scott's dad wasn't a lover of water, didn't understand its allure, how it hypnotized and seduced Alice. He always saw the danger, never the beauty.

After the little boy on the beach had run headlong into the water, his father scooped him up and swung him high in the air. Their conjoined laughter carried across the beach, conjuring memories of early motherhood for Alice. It had been a sweet, innocent time. All-consuming and, at the same time, fleeting.

How well she remembered searching for sharks' teeth on the beach with Scott when he was small. Their special summer ritual.

"Keep a sharp eye out," Alice would encourage her frustrated toddler. "You'll find one soon."

He'd dart back and forth, breathlessly picking up rocks and bits of tar from the sand and then stomp his tiny feet as his hopes were dashed yet again.

And then, after straining their eyes and finding nothing, the glistening, fossilized teeth began to appear like black jellybeans on the sand. They materialized as if conjured by a little boy's optimistic longing. Alice and Scott would fill their fists and pockets and carry their haul back to rinse off under the hose at the edge of the sand. Then Scott's dad would get interested and help them catalog their treasures by size, color and shape. It was a rare family moment of shared pleasure.

Older than Alice by nearly 20 years, Scott's dad remembered collecting arrowheads in the woods where he grew up in the 1950s. The sharks' teeth of Scott's childhood were the coastal version of the Lenape and Susquehannock artifacts his father had scavenged in north central Pennsylvania. Alice loved the purity of Scott's connection with his dad. Nothing forced or orchestrated, just the natural bond of father and son, in the before times.

After the divorce, those golden moments were few and far between.

Scott's dad drilled a hole in an especially large shark's tooth—no doubt a megalodon—they all agreed. Alice strung it on a leather cord, and her boy had worn it proudly on his tawny bare chest all summer long.

As she savored the cherished memory of her son and his father, Alice noticed two older women, stooped and stiff, crowned with floppy sunhats. Their swimsuits were more like soggy dresses. Their skin hung in folds and puddled around their knees and elbows as they made their way down the beach. Their upper arms looked like empty tube socks. Brown as nuts and stout as beer cans, the women plodded along in companionable silence. Alice wondered if she was so far removed from them after all. And she felt a sudden kindness toward them, a recognition of sorts.

She glanced at the mottled skin on her legs. She'd been hoping her age spots would grow together into a tan. Where were the strong, supple limbs of her youth and even her early middle age? Her fingers went absently to her crepey cleavage that only a couple of years ago had been smooth and firm. She sighed deeply and mentally affirmed her worth, despite her gently aging body. *You are not your looks. You are not your looks.*

But growing up Southern and female had instilled a sort of inadvertent shallowness in Alice. Years of turning heads with just a look over her shoulder or a toss of her hair had taken its toll. And she was her own worst critic, seeing tiny flaws invisible to others. Scott would bemoan her self-deprecating remarks. *Mom, you're not fat. Mom, you're not old. You're so hard on yourself. Stop it.*

And yet, nothing is harder than to let go of what you once took for granted.

Then Alice remembered she wouldn't live to see her flesh wither and droop with age.

She stood slowly and shook the sand from her lap. She stretched her arms overhead and arched her back like a cat, only wincing a little at the sharp stab of pain that was becoming her near-constant companion.

As Alice made her way back to the cottage, Tabitha manifested out of nowhere and serpentined between Alice's legs, tail held high, mewing softly. *Oh, to have the exquisite confidence and poise of a cat, marveled Alice. Ageless, ever-graceful, fully present.*

Glancing down to stroke Tabitha's cottony fur and snatch at her feathery tail, Alice was astonished by the tiny plants growing among the rocks and driftwood. Their sheer determination to live despite their inhospitable surroundings. Did she feel that same urge? Maybe she'd rather float through life, like spongy, brown sargassum, and let the current guide her path. No compass, no schedule, no to-do list, just the constant motion of the ocean.

CHAPTER 6

Alice and Evangeline had always been caregivers, as most women are. Over the years, Alice had taken care of two husbands and various stepchildren, her aging parents, and her own son. Evangeline cared for her elderly grandmother, tended the intergenerational joy and grief of her Gullah ancestors, and watched over the little tribe of Kennesaw Islanders, like a protective matriarch. Maybe that's why the two women bonded over loggerhead sea turtles. Alice and Evangeline's innate nurturing instincts kicked in to protect this ancient species and to shepherd its vulnerable offspring into the sea.

Kennesaw Island is the epicenter of sea turtle rescue and rehabilitation in Georgia's Golden Isles. Volunteers patrol the barrier island beaches at night in search of nesting loggerheads all summer long, leading up to the annual hatch in August. Although Alice moved to the island just after the season, Evangeline had spent months indoctrinating her new friend in the mysterious ways of mother turtles, who returned year after year to Kennesaw to lay their precious eggs, sometimes as many as six nests of one hundred eggs each.

The loggerheads are an endangered species, susceptible to the incidental hazards of fishing gear and boat propellers. If they can avoid getting tangled up in nets and obstructed by other man-made obstacles, sea turtles can live as long as sixty years. The intrepid creatures return to the exact spot where they were born to mate and lay their own eggs. Their sense of place is strong, and home is always calling them back from the sea.

Nesting mother sea turtles are said to go into a trance while laying their eggs, shedding salty tears in the process, although they're likely just excreting excess salt from the special glands in the corners of their eyes. Alice much preferred the idea of turtles crying, as Evangeline described it.

"The mothers are so overcome with emotion and the effort of laying their eggs, they cry tears of joy and hope for the children they will never know," Evangeline opined, in her own trance-like state as she spun another of her island stories. Alice was always spellbound.

"They know they won't be around to help their babies grow up, and it breaks their hearts."

After the mother turtles lay multiple clutches of eggs in the sand, they drag themselves back into the ocean and don't look back.

"Perhaps they say a little prayer to the Moon Goddess to watch over their young and guide them safely to the sea," suggested Evangeline.

The lives of baby sea turtles are, in fact, fraught with peril, and prayers for their safe passage are encouraged. If the eggs aren't eaten by predators, which include raccoons, dogs and housecats, the hatchlings use a temporary, claw-like egg tooth to crack themselves out of their shells. Then they rest up for the next leg of their arduous journey.

After they've regained their strength, the baby turtles do the most amazing thing—they work together to burrow up through the sand, pausing near the surface to wait for nightfall, making it less likely they will be picked off by seagulls, ghost crabs and lizards on their mad dash to the sea. Their shells are still soft, making them especially vulnerable. As they scurry along the beach, they imprint with the sand, forming a connection so they can return years later.

Only one in a thousand hatchlings will survive to adulthood.

Alice was dismayed by the way the mother turtles abandoned their unborn babies. It seemed cruel and unfeeling. And yet, these complex creatures have survived, essentially unchanged, for over a hundred million years. Against all odds, they have persevered.

Evangeline was part of a designated beach patrol and began taking Alice along on her nightly expeditions to monitor turtle activity and watch over the eggs during their incubation period. As tourists and summer folk made their way back to Kennesaw, Evangeline would hand out red cellophane and gently remind them to cover their flashlights and phones so as not to confuse and startle the nesting turtles or disturb the eggs. She and Alice used yellow tape to cordon off the nests.

Back at the bookstore, Evangeline and Alice had hosted a baby shower of sorts for this season's hatchlings, featuring a curated collection of books on conservation and habitat preservation. Evangeline had invited specialists from the turtle rehab center to discuss the delicate marine and marshland ecosystem of Kennesaw Island and the important role the turtles played in maintaining it.

Alice had created a pillowed book nook for the children who attended. While they snacked on turtle-shaped sugar cookies they had decorated themselves, Alice read aloud from Douglas Wood's sumptuously illustrated fable about God and humanity's impact on the planet and the wisdom of a wise old turtle.

… the people listened, and began to hear …
And to see God in one another
… and in the beauty of all the Earth.
And Old Turtle smiled.

Sometimes the eggs never hatched, or the nests were raided by predators or unwittingly ruined by careless humans partying in the dunes. But one glorious night, Alice witnessed the most marvelous thing. She and Evangeline were making their rounds on a routine Turtle Walk. The nests were clearly marked, and the countdown had begun to when baby turtles were expected. Evangeline said their chances were good to witness a hatchling release, but you just never know.

The sand felt cool underfoot in the late summer, and Alice

marveled that she had been "on island" for almost a year. She had renewed her six-month lease and extended it to a year this time. The owners weren't planning to visit this summer and seemed happy with the arrangement. Alice wasn't thinking about the future so much as living in the moment.

She felt strong from all the beach walks, despite losing weight. Her appetite had tapered off as the cancer progressed, but she still savored salty mussels and fresh-caught shrimp, dry white wine, and Kennesaw Island's special soft-serve ice cream.

Evangeline whispered turtle wisdom as the moon rose overhead. Alice thought about how she would never know her grandchildren or see them grow up. How she would miss out on smelling their sweet baby scalps and patting them gently on the back as she sang to them just as she had to Scott. She would not see them run laughing on the beach like Skye, her surrogate daughter, inner child, island faery. And she felt suddenly sad and tired.

Just then they stopped dead in their tracks, Evangeline softly touching Alice's arm. Alice looked toward her friend who raised a finger to her lips and then pointed to the sand pit in front of them, where tiny, shiny turtles were emerging, as if from quicksand, stacking their empty egg shells to propel themselves to the surface of the nest, when they moved as one, like a school of fish or birds in flight, their little flippers working fast and furiously. And then they were up and out and scurrying down the gentle slope of the beach toward the ocean. The rising tide reached out to greet them, extending its frothy piano fingers, playing a timeless tune only the turtles could hear. The creatures were simultaneously fragile and strong, trusting their instincts, against all odds, driven by their ferocity to survive, despite their vulnerability.

Do they even know how precarious their little lives are, wondered Alice to herself. *How they're teetering between life and death on a sandy tightrope?*

Alice looked on in awe, as she felt Evangeline's warm, calloused hand in hers. And then her other hand was clasped by a smaller, cooler palm. She glanced down to see Skye standing beside her, eyes full of wonder, as the three of them witnessed the life-affirming miracle.

CHAPTER 7

It was the morning after witnessing the flight of the turtles that Alice staggered home just as the sun was coming up over the Mermaid Cottage. She and Evangeline had stopped for coffee at Island Brew, but it wasn't open yet, so Alice tumbled out of the jeep and in the front door in a noctambulous stupor. She was simultaneously exhausted and exhilarated, almost tripping over Tabitha who met her in the hall with fretful meows and insistent head rubs. Alice walked zombie-like into the kitchen, turning on the tea kettle as she fumbled for the cat food. Once she had a steaming cup in her hand and Tabitha was happily munching her meal, Alice wandered out to the porch and plopped down gratefully into the swing.

So much to think about. A year on Kennesaw. Where had the time gone? And how much did she have left?

She thought about Evangeline, island goddess, mystical, spiritual being, friend. Alice had to tell her. It wasn't fair not to. She resolved to do it. Soon. Well, soonish.

And Finn, what of Finn? They'd fallen into a comfortable rhythm over the last several months. Quiet meals at the Mermaid Cottage that they threw together with whatever was on hand. Finn would bring wine. Alice would toss pasta into boiling water and unseal the mason jars of tomatoes Finn had canned when the last of his precious Purple Skyes had ripened. They'd walk on the beach for hours. He joined her in her frequent naps, never commenting on her increasingly prominent hipbones as his hands moved over her body in careful caresses.

Surely, he knew she wasn't well, Alice told herself. But even as she said it in her mind, she knew it was a lie. Finn was the king of compartmentalization. It was his superpower and the key to his survival.

She remembered at Christmas when they'd strung lights around the empty hearth and sipped chilled champagne. Finn had scavenged for logs in the scrubby woods around the house and was working to build a fire. Alice watched from her cozy nest on the sofa. She and Tabitha were piled up with quilts and blankets. The cottage wasn't well insulated, and the air was cold and salty as the fire caught with snaps and crackles, punctuated by pops. The wood was still damp.

Finn looked over his shoulder and smiled irresistibly, as he brushed the soot and dust from his faded denim-clad knees. Just for a moment, he seemed carefree and happy, like he'd temporarily shed the invisible cloak of sadness he often wore. Shrugged it right off his shoulders.

I could fall in love with this guy. In fact, maybe I already have.

They talked easily, except about their feelings for each other. Somehow, that was too hard. Too precarious for their damaged hearts to take. So, they showed how much they cared for each other instead. Acts of service had always been Alice's love language. Having Finn putter around the house and fix the leaky faucet in the kitchen sink and sweep the back porch without being asked— that was enough for her. And his eyes told her more than words ever could.

For the first time in a long time, she felt loved.

In fact, Finn was beyond smitten. He was deeply in love with Alice, whether he knew it or not. As he settled in under the blankets with her on Christmas Eve and every time since then, he felt content. Peaceful. Like the past couldn't hurt him anymore and like all the tragedy and heartache of his life had led him to her.

And so, it came to be that Alice and Finn were a couple, much to the chagrin of Kennesaw's cadre of single women, islanders and tourists alike, from the Laughing Lotus Lulu-clad yoginis to the dangerously diamonded divorcees who frequented the bar of the Driftwood Kitchen, where Finn was known to sip his single-malt, gazing distractedly into its amber depths, oblivious to the hair flips and crossing and uncrossing of bare legs around him.

Finn started saying no to the dinner invitations in Atlanta and leaving right after his meetings to drive back to Kennesaw, eager to see Alice. They were reading a book together, about past lives. He listened to the audio version while poring over legal documents. Alice was always amazed at his cerebral multitasking. She preferred to consume content the old-fashioned way, propping an actual book on her knees, turning the pages at her own pace.

And Alice wondered if she had known Finn in a previous lifetime. She'd once done a past-life regression therapy at a wellness retreat in the Tucson desert. An auburn-haired Scottish healing arts practitioner named Rae Jessie led the far-out spa treatment. Alice didn't know quite what to expect but surrendered herself to the experience, despite Rae Jessie's annoying habit of referring to herself in the third person.

Eyes closed, reclining on a velvet cushion, and clutching a black malachite stone to her chest for protection, Alice let go and fell down the rabbit hole. Malachite is known as the stone of transformation, thought to reveal and heal emotional pain by absorbing it. Rae Jessie suggested that malachite also warded off traumatic memories so that the exercise would only be positive.

Alice followed the woman's verbal cues and traveled back in time. She found herself barefoot in soft, green grass in some sort of Elizabethan dress with a laced corset over a loose-fitting blouse. There was an arched bridge nearby, and Alice was aware of the sound of water running under it. It was like a scene from the movie "Shakespeare in Love."

In her regression, Alice was still a child, innocent and free, not yet on the cusp of puberty or self-awareness. A young boy ran toward her laughing and held out his hand. He was wearing a leather vest and breeches and was also barefoot. His eyes were warm, his expression guileless, his smile genuine and kind.

"C'mon," he said.

She took his hand, and they were off, on an adventure that transcended time and space, that was real and dear and authentic. Comfortable in their skin and in each other's presence. An unspoken secret shared between them. No agenda. No ulterior motive. No fear.

It was the essence of love.

CHAPTER 8

Alice awoke with a start from a fitful sleep. The sun was already streaming through the lace panels on her bedroom window, the early-morning breeze having given way to mid-morning humidity and stillness. Why hadn't Tabitha awakened her, she wondered groggily. Moving slowly, Alice swung her stiff legs over the side of the bed and sat there for a moment. She looked at the warm golden floorboards and at her bony feet. Toenails painted white. The color was called "Dazzling Diamonds," and she and Skye had painted each other's nails with it, giggling and watching the sparkly polish glint in the sunshine as they dangled their feet from the porch swing. The memory made Alice smile, despite the dull ache in her bones. Speaking of which, she felt knobby now, too thin.

You can't be too thin or too rich. Wasn't that how the saying went?

But when Alice took in her skinny arms and her hip bones silhouetted by her cotton gown as she stood and stretched, she thought maybe there was such a thing as too thin. It had been a year since she came to Kennesaw. Time was running out. And she still had not told Finn her prognosis.

As she wrapped her terrycloth robe around herself and cinched the thick belt tightly at her waist, she strode purposefully into the kitchen. Today would be the day. She and Finn were going to get coffee (which for her meant a chai latte with oat milk, no water, and cinnamon powder steamed in and on top) after yoga. She would tell him something. What that something was, she didn't yet know.

Pouring water in her teapot, Alice raised her eyes to the sea, her spiritual home, her compass, her heartbeat. It was then that she noticed Skye and Tabitha on the beach playing. Skye was wearing blue and white seersucker shorts and no shirt. She was dancing to some music only she could hear, spinning in circles, arms flung wide. Tabitha was batting at her feet with plush paws and then skedaddling away in gremlin mode, which is what Alice called it when her generally chill old girl went all Halloween cat, arched back, puffed out tail, sidestepping like a crab.

Those shorts looked so familiar. Alice couldn't place them at first. A long-forgotten memory tugged at the edges of her brain, hovering there just out of reach, like Skye's ankles to Tabitha's swatting paws.

And then it came flooding back to her. A summer evening, when Alice was a little girl, fierce and feisty and brave, just like Skye. She and her best friend, Tricinda Wells—*wasn't it funny how you thought of childhood friends in terms of their first and last name, Alice thought to herself*—had been climbing trees and swinging on the metal swing set in Alice's backyard. Barefoot and tan. Scraped and bruised. But oblivious and giddily in the moment, as children so often are.

Alice's time with Tricinda was fleeting. They'd been neighbors only briefly when Alice's dad was temporarily transferred to Springfield, Tenn., before moving back to Georgia. Hence the friendship was frozen in memory, suspended in amber in Alice's mind.

Higher and higher the two girls swung, pumping their legs, and leaning back in the swings, letting the wind catch their hair in its arms. It had felt very daring to take off the sleeveless seersucker shirt that buttoned up the front. It matched her shorts. Tricinda was a tomboy and less inhibited. She happily pulled her purple T-shirt over her head and said, *let's pretend we're boys.*

It wasn't a gender identity thing like nowadays. It was a declaration of independence. It was freedom. When Alice was growing up, girls were still supposed to be sugar and spice and everything nice. Not shirtless wildlings running amok. But oh, how Alice longed to run amok. She still remembered the thrill of it. Swinging in the fading sunlight on a carefree summer evening. The lightening bugs, dusk's winged darlings, were just starting to blink.

Of course, the mood was ruined when Alice's little brother came out and said, *you can't take your shirt off. You're a girl. I'm telling.* He'd run squealing toward the house, yelling *Mommy, Mommy, Mommy* at the top of his lungs. Alice had given chase but had run smack into the seesaw and knocked the wind out of herself. She could still feel the surprised *oof* as she hit the metal bar that held the wooden plank. It was darkish, and she hadn't seen it as she flew across the grass in hot pursuit. Even now, as she recalled the moment, she felt a searing pain in her abdomen and closed her eyes, playing her hands on her belly.

She could still see the lightening bugs hovering lazily overhead as she lay stunned in the grass.

Why was Skye wearing Alice's shorts? Or shorts just like Alice wore as a child?

Alice was thinking about her childhood memory and Skye's wardrobe and all the things as she sat in lotus practicing ujjayi breathing after a particularly challenging vinyasa practice. Ujjayi breath or "breath of victory" or "ocean breath" is a sequence of inhalations and exhalations through the nose, with your tongue touching the roof of your mouth, while you simultaneously engage your energy locks or bhandas. It's extremely challenging and extremely beneficial.

You make a sound with your breath like the sound you hear when you hold a conch shell up to your ear. Alice never ceased to be amazed by that sound, whether coming from the shell or from deep within herself.

She and Finn were discussing it after yoga at Island Brew, over flakey chocolate croissants. Alice knew she had to tell him she had cervical cancer that had metastasized. That she was dying. That she didn't know how long they had together but how she wanted to savor every moment. She wanted to thank him for these last months on Kennesaw Island that would be the last months of her life.

But as she looked up from her steamy cup with the swirling

clouds in it, she saw something in his eyes that looked like hope and love all mixed together. And she just couldn't do it. So, she did something even worse.

Finn was driving back to Atlanta. He'd thrown some clothes in a bag and headed out right after Alice broke up with him. She'd offered no explanation whatsoever. It was as though the last year on the island had never happened. Did he dream it? Was he mistaken when they made love, and he felt a closeness to her he had never experienced with anyone else and thought she felt it, too?

She had given him no reason. No warning. Just blindsided him over coffee. Said she didn't want to see him anymore, no wait, that she *couldn't* see him anymore, whatever that meant.

I love you but I have to let you go.

Just like Sarah. Just like Lucy. Just like everything good in his life. Just like that.

He arrived at the condo, soulless and barren, just as he'd left it. As he opened the door, he noticed a note had been slipped underneath it. When he unsealed the blank envelope and unfolded the card, he was hit by a wave of nostalgia. The creamy stationery felt familiar. Then he saw the handwriting and felt the second gut punch of the day.

Finn, I'm in town and I need to see you.

Sarah

That was it. One sentence, with a new phone number scrawled under her name. He didn't immediately recognize the area code. When had she left the note? Was she still in town? And more importantly, what was he going to do about it?

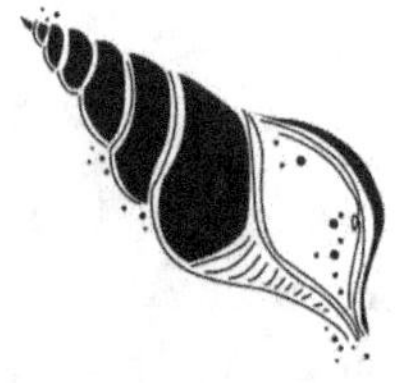

CHAPTER 9

Finn was sitting at the bar of an upscale Atlanta restaurant, staring into his single-malt Scotch when Sarah arrived. He happened to turn and look toward the door just as she walked in, and time almost stood still. It was as if she were walking in slow motion. She tossed her lovely dark hair over her shoulder as she paused to look around the dimly lit bar for him, her eyes adjusting to the low lights in the mahogany-paneled room. Her red slip of a dress hugged her athletic figure in all the right places. It was as if she hadn't aged a day in all these years.

It wasn't until she sat down beside him, as he pulled the tall chair out for her, that Finn noticed the lines on Sarah's face. Not laugh lines but deep furrows of sadness, between her brows and at the corners of her slightly downturned mouth. He saw it immediately. She was still beautiful. Still broken.

"Hey, stranger," she said simply.

Finn motioned for the bartender.

"Still vodka rocks?" he asked softly. She nodded.

They took their drinks to a quiet booth and slid in. After just a moment's awkwardness and small talk, Finn and Sarah became themselves again, comfortable in each other's presence, connected by the profound happiness of their time together and the sludgy shared sorrow that ended it. Lucy was an ethereal butterfly flitting around the periphery of their conversation, always present but just out of sight. Fluttering wings and a flash of color. Then gone.

They began to unfold the layers of their lives over the past decade. Sarah had traveled non-stop, keeping her demons at bay with overseas stints of pro-bono legal work. That and her practice had shifted to helping parents adopt foreign children. Helping them navigate the paperwork and bureaucracy and bullshit.

She was still running, figuratively and literally, miles and miles. While she didn't compete anymore, she still ran daily. It was her moving meditation, her escape, her drug.

Sarah had never let go of Lucy, of course. Never would. And although there had been other men in her life, they were never *the one*. Never Finn. Contrary to the rumors, she had not had another child. In fact, she had her tubes tied to ensure that she never would.

But the work she was doing helping children find parents and helping parents find children was healing her heart. In fact, she had been in Croatia, advocating on behalf of an American couple who desperately wanted a little girl. Okaysana was tiny and malnourished and splintered in spirit. Just a wisp of a girl. But the moment when she met her adoptive parents for the first time was transformative. She stood up a little taller, her frail shoulders visibly relaxing. It was as though the constant ache for what she knew she was missing finally vanished.

Finn and Sarah knew that ache. While Sarah had found purpose and meaning in making new families whole, Finn had buried his pain in work and liquor. He had closed himself off to connections. Kept his fractured heart safely stored away in a secret compartment. Until Alice had appeared that day in the Beachcomber, and he'd felt something for the first time in ages. It was a lightness, like fog lifting when the sun warms the sand.

And now she'd pushed him away, too. Just like Sarah had so many years ago.

Three drinks in, Finn finally asked, "Why are you here, Sarah? Why now?"

She answered in five words. Five words that spoke volumes. "I want to try again."

Alice and Evangeline were walking on the beach, empty wine glasses in hand. Alice had called her friend and asked her to come over for supper, a meal she had picked at and not eaten. Her loss of appetite had not gone unnoticed.

"What's going on, Alice?" asked Evangeline.

Alice spilled the whole story of breaking up with Finn for no good reason and seeing the dark cloud fall over his face. How he had gotten up from the table at Island Brew and quietly walked out the door, not even looking back. She'd tried to call him, but he hadn't answered. Her babbling texts were ignored. She wanted to take it all back, but she couldn't. He had trusted her, and she had intentionally wounded him, because she was too afraid to tell him the truth.

"I'm sick, E," Alice said dully.

"Sick in the head, girl," countered Evangeline. "Finn is a good man. And he loves you. What were you even thinking?" She stopped in her tracks and turned to face Alice.

"No, *really* sick. I'm dying," said Alice simply. "I've been dying since I got here."

And she told Evangeline everything that was on her heart. Her fear and loneliness came pouring out. She was afraid of letting Finn down. Of being a burden to Scott. Of relying too much on Evangeline. Of abandoning Tabitha. Alice stopped just short of mentioning Skye. That was a secret she would take to her grave.

Then they were walking again. Back to the cottage. Dolly, the carved mermaid figurehead, stood majestically in the sand as they approached. She was illuminated by the setting sun.

"I know, sweetie, I know," was all Evangeline had said.

And she did know. Had known for a long time. Had watched her friend waste away, seen the hollows under her eyes. But had also seen her radiance. Alice had bloomed on Kennesaw, even as she was dying from the inside out. Evangeline had seen her transformed by the magic of the island. Alice seemed to drink it in, the sea air, the surf, the precious miracle of the turtles. It was as though she had metamorphosized into this ethereal being, her body and spirit enhanced by her increasing fragility.

They hugged and cried as they sat in the swing together.

Tabitha kept a restless vigil at the end of the porch, tail twitching. And Skye sat in the darkness just beneath the porch absorbing the conversation, her thin back pressed against the latticework so long it left a mark, like a giant doily on her skin.

Evangeline sleepwalked around the bookstore. She was distracted and troubled by her conversation with Alice. Not because Alice was sick. Evangeline had always known that on some level. Rather, she was disappointed that Alice had thrown away her chance at happiness with both hands. And crushed Finn's soul in the process. It had been such a blessing to see him come back to life after all these years—to see him literally go from grey to living color again.

She well remembered him with Sarah and Lucy and how golden they were together, like a glowing love bubble. And then it all came apart. But when Alice arrived on Kennesaw, there was an energetic shift. Evangeline suspected that Alice was not aware of her own powers. Her ingenuous empathy. Her capacity to love completely. It was remarkable really, after all she had been through. That she was still open to beautiful expressions of profound emotions. Most people closed their hearts tight like clam shells, after getting them broken. Finn had.

Whether she knew it or not, Alice was remarkably resilient, in Evangeline's opinion. And brave.

Because we are all broken inside. And no one else can heal us. This was something Evangeline had known as a child. Something her grandmother had taught her without trying to. It wasn't a life lesson in sadness. It was the secret to happiness.

Growing up without a mother or a father, Evangeline had felt inherently other, like a changeling or an orphan, even though she had her grandmother to care for her. She begged Granny Annie not to have to go to church on Mother's Day, when the ushers would offer a red rose or a white rose to pin on your lapel, signifying whether your mother was living or dead. Of course, her grandmother made her go. Even though she was the only child in the congregation wearing a white rose on the tucked bodice of her

Sunday dress. For one thing, Granny Annie didn't put up with any foolishness when it came to worship. For another thing, she knew if she let Evangeline hide from her pain, it would fester inside.

"You heal yourself, honey. That's all there is to it. You heal yourself," her grandmother said simply, as she took Evangeline's face in her warm hands and gently wiped away the tears with her thumbs.

Evangeline had done it, and she'd watched Alice and Finn do it, too. They probably thought they fixed each other or "completed" each other in some way. Evangeline didn't believe that for a minute. Because she knew that God brings people into your life when you're ready and not before. And that you *choose* to be happy or not.

It's the ultimate empowerment. Your life. Your choice. Your happiness.

"We are fragile vessels, child, buffeted about by the waves," Granny Annie was fond of saying. "And waves are just energy traveling through water. The trick is to harness that energy and calm the water. Steal the chaos from the sea and use it for your own magic."

Evangeline had stilled her own personal tsunami long ago, with the sheer force of her will and the loving guidance of her grandmother.

She shook her head as she reshelved books and wondered why people chose heartache over happiness again and again.

Then Evangeline picked up her phone and called Finn.

He was already in the car when Evangeline called. Finn had left Atlanta for good. After that third drink with Sarah. He knew he wouldn't be back. They'd cried and hugged and wished each other the happiness they knew they couldn't find together.

Because they had been good together before Lucy died. And now, they were good on their own. And through their tears, Finn and Sarah could finally see that. They could forgive each other and themselves and celebrate their beautiful child and reminisce about her magical laugh and her sweet baby smell. Her tangled cornsilk corkscrews and her love of the ocean.

I had to try, Finn, you know?

I know, sweetheart. I know.

I miss her every single day. And it's like I feel guilty for being happy sometimes. But then I see her in the eyes of these children. Our little girl, and I know she's gone but it's like she's still here for just a moment. And those moments are everything. They sustain me, you know? Like I could live on them. And I think maybe it's okay to be okay.

Finn replayed his conversation with Sarah over and over in his head. Closure was a tenuous thing. It came and went like clouds skimming over the sea. But seeing Sarah and knowing that she was okay was the closest Finn had come. To letting her go with love. And to giving himself permission to get on with his life.

And his life was on Kennesaw now. He'd figure out the details later. Shutting down his practice, maybe putting out a shingle on the island and helping the locals with business contracts and building permits, trust funds and property transfers. He could be an old-school family-practice lawyer. It sounded so simple and felt so right. He'd commit and go all in, rather than holding back and splitting himself between two worlds.

And he'd get her back. Alice, that is.

When Evangeline explained about Alice's cancer, Finn's analytical mind immediately went into problem-solving mode. His worldview didn't allow for a world without Alice in it.

CHAPTER 10

Alice didn't sleep much anymore. It was like the veil between sleeping and being awake had been pierced somehow. Days bled into nights, and wakefulness was a peculiar state. It was as though she was in a constant state of dreaming. It wasn't entirely unpleasant. In fact, it took the edge off things, including her breakup with Finn, which was utterly devastating. Like letting go of hope. But being alone felt familiar and safe. Heartbreak was an old friend.

And Alice convinced herself that she had done it out of kindness for Finn, rather than out of fear of losing control, of being vulnerable, like those tiny loggerhead turtles, all soft shelled and exposed. She'd rather be David the cat and curl up under a trashcan in the neighbor's yard than risk being needy. It had always been this way with Alice. As much as she was a caregiver and loved to help and nurture others, she was afraid to need help. Afraid to want love, or accept it, for fear it wouldn't be real. Wouldn't last. Because isn't it better to long for something you've never had than to have it and lose it?

These were the thoughts swirling through Alice's mind as she half sleepwalked along the beach, Tabitha trailing in her wake, making furry figure eights around Alice's legs, almost but not quite tripping her. Until she did. Alice stumbled and fell hard, catching herself with her hands in the surf, the sand crumbling away from her grasp as the tide tiptoed back out to sea.

It was then that Alice noticed the sky was strange. Changing colors even though it was the middle of the night, nowhere near daybreak. These solitary strolls were Alice's alternative to sleep, which had become nearly impossible due to the pain. If she kept moving, she could focus on all the nighttime wonders of the sand and sea rather than her throbbing bones. Once her eyes adjusted to the darkness, she saw tiny sea crabs scuttling across the wet packed beach as the tide receded, their little lairs suddenly revealed until the next wave came crashing in. She smiled as she thought of that magical evening with Evangeline, the both of them watching like proud mamas as the baby sea turtles hatched and made their way to the sea. She thought about Scott, her own baby, all grown up and on his way in the world. She missed him fiercely, as only a mother can miss her child, but that ache was tempered by a deep sense of well-being. She knew her job was done with her son. He had become a fine young man. He would go on to do great things, of this she was certain. But she wouldn't be there to bear witness.

The night sky wasn't pitch black dotted by stars as it sometimes was in the time between midnight and dawn. It wasn't yet letting go of the darkness to reveal the sherbet shades of sunrise. It was something else entirely—it was purple. She tasted the color with her eyes and considered it. Aubergine, plum maybe, an inky dark indigo. Like an intense cabernet sauvignon, full-bodied and foreboding. Then, as she watched, the sky began to glow and vibrate like a school of neons flashing as one across the water of her childhood aquarium.

Alice remembered Evangeline's haunting description of the night Lucy disappeared.

Bioluminescence, it's called. When the ocean blooms with tiny phytoplankton that blanket the water, turning it the color of dried blood by day. At night, it's an iridescent blue.

It was then she turned her eyes to the sea. It had, indeed, transmuted into a dazzling fluorescent shade of blue. Again, she thought of the distinctive stripe on her beloved tank-bound neon tetras. But this was something else entirely, the surface of the water was emanating an otherworldly light. She thought of Skye's tutu as she danced on the driftwood, or was it Lucy's tutu that washed up on the shore days after her disappearance?

Alice stood and faced the roiling ocean. The rainbowlike refraction of light waves that made the water glow was reflecting on the shore, illuminating jewel-like specks in the sand. Shark's teeth, Alice thought immediately, but no, the colors were too vivid. As she glanced around, she saw emerald-green, honey-brown, icy-white, and aquamarine nuggets of sea glass winking improbably at her like discarded driftwood dragon eyes or maybe shed mermaid scales.

Then Alice waded into the velvet sea. She stood stock still as the bite of the cold tide washed suddenly over her feet, grabbing her pajamas like a mischievous partner pulling her onto a crowded dance floor. She took another step into the water, as Tabitha hissed a warning behind her. But Alice didn't hear her old cat calling out. She heard, instead, the siren's call of the sea. She let her robe drop from around her shoulders and pulled her T-shirt over her head. As she strode deeper into the waves, she adjusted to the chill and was invigorated by it. She swam right out of her pajama bottoms, and each movement of her arms caused a halo effect of iridescence as the microscopic algae glowed from the disturbance.

Alice felt no pain now, only an inexplicable joy and lightness. The water was a caress against her skin. She breast-stroked her way to the deep, frog kicking her legs behind her, then switching instinctively to a dolphin kick as she impulsively dove beneath the surface. Alice was unable to see at first, but all her other senses were alive, guiding her further and further from shore. When she surfaced, she flipped over and floated on her back, riding the gentle rise and fall of the glowing waves, staring up at the purple sky. She felt incredibly calm and unafraid. Like she was home.

Did she doze? Could you fall asleep while floating on the ocean in a swath of fluorescent algae? Alice wasn't sure. It felt like she was dreaming though, or perhaps recalling happy memories and moments. A montage of images swam before her closed eyes. When Scott was little, when she herself was a young girl. The smell of blown-out birthday candles. The giddy, dangerous feeling of being tossed high in the air and then safely caught in strong arms.

Laughter, warmth, love. The ocean became a womb enveloping her, and Alice didn't seem to notice that she was no longer floating on the surface. She was sinking now into its welcoming depths. And that was when she saw Skye again.

Alice was completely submerged, and yet, she wasn't consciously holding her breath. She opened her eyes and rather than murkiness, she saw everything clearly. There was Skye, her wild seaweed hair suspended around her, her sun-kissed skin glowing in the subterranean light. The little girl took Alice's hand, and together they swam down deeper into kelp forests, among the rocks. Alice noticed Skye's luminous skin gave way to scales just below her waist and became a lovely blue-green aquamarine sheath instead of legs and ended in a magnificent fishtail. The little selkie was leading her to a place she'd never been before. Instead of being afraid, Alice was utterly enchanted.

She lost track of time as Skye showed her the otherworldly wonders beneath the surface. She saw turtles and sharks, starfish, and rays swimming in the night sea.

Instead of feeling her own pain, both physical and emotional, she was able to focus on the absolute miracle of life around her. Skye stopped now and motioned for Alice to look at what she thought was a pile of rocks. But as she stared she saw first one eye, then two staring back. She could just make out a suction-cup covered arm curled around the rocks and realized she was face to face with a lovely little octopus, one of the smartest and most misunderstood of all the ocean's creatures. As she watched it watching her, she marveled as it transformed from a sand-colored and textured blob, indistinguishable from its surroundings, into a smooth, crimson creature, the color of a beating heart.

Alice held out her hand, and the cephalopod wrapped an arm around her wrist, gently learning her and teaching her at the same time. Compassion. Empathy. Acceptance. So many intense emotions pulsed between them. Alice felt seen, heard and understood.

They went on like this for hours—or was it days—Alice and Skye, exploring the subterranean depths, swimming together underwater until Alice could almost feel her own mermaid tail propelling her forward instead of human legs. They didn't eat or sleep or surface. They simply existed in oneness with the ocean. Alice was content in a way she'd never known before. She and Skye communicated with gestures and expressions and perhaps even their minds. Then Skye gently pointed upward and took Alice's hand as they swam toward the light.

The last sound Alice heard was the distinctive whistle-like cry Skye made as she breached the surface of the water through the churning froth. The South Korean Haenyeo, the free divers of Jeju, call it "sumbisori."

Then Alice was wrapped in Mylar blankets and being lifted onto a pallet. The lights of the phosphorescent ocean had been replaced by the flashing lights of an ambulance. There were people rushing all around, their frenetic motions set against the crackle of walkie-talkies and cawing gulls. Alice felt removed from it all somehow, as if she were still underwater or just on the other side of a dream. Everything was happening in slow motion.

It was then she noticed someone was holding her hand, and she looked up past the paramedics to see Finn's worried face just over her own. She smiled with her eyes, because her nose and mouth were under an oxygen mask. She saw his expression relax just a little and the endearing crinkles around his eyes deepen slightly. As they loaded her into the back of the ambulance and went about buckling her in and attaching various monitors and bags of fluids, Finn stayed right beside her, just in her line of sight. She wanted to tell him where she'd been and what she'd seen, but the effort of speech was too much.

"I thought I'd lost you," Finn said softly, as he brushed a lock of wet hair off her forehead, his warm hand lingering on her pale, cold skin. It felt like a kiss.

And in that moment, Alice realized that her aloneness, the solitary life she had come to know, was becoming something else entirely. And that her sickness, which Finn didn't yet know about— or so she thought—was something they could face together. She didn't have to hide her cancer, like a character flaw to be despised and buried away. Life, death, whatever came, it didn't matter. Everything was going to be okay. And Skye had brought her back to this side of the world, reuniting her with Finn, and making them whole in a way they hadn't been before, living their own parallel broken lives.

They didn't need each other to complete themselves. They chose each other once they felt complete. And by mending their own wounded psyches, Alice and Finn made a safe, healthy place to grow a new love. Fully present in the moment. Without fear or worry for the future.

That little angel mermaid, ghost creature, caught in the seam between two universes had helped them heal their splintered hearts by bringing them together. Because shared grief is a lighter burden to carry. And hope manifests when you let go of pain. And trust can only come from absolute vulnerability. Two souls, shedding their skins.

Lucy had done that for her father. Skye had done it for her friend.

Finally, Alice was well and truly home.

A Word from the Author

And now, dear reader, *Thank you!* Thank you for giving your time to read this book. It means a lot that you trusted me as a storyteller to entertain and hopefully inspire you with this story. Stories need an audience, and I appreciate you being my audience for just a little while. Again, thank you.

Now I'd like to ask a favor—and I know this is a big request—if you enjoyed the story of Alice, and Skye, and Evangeline, and Finn and the others, would you consider leaving a review wherever you bought this book or on your favorite social media platform? I'd love for as many readers as possible to discover this story, and your voice can help do that.

Leave a review and tell a friend! Word-of-mouth is still the best way to introduce this story to other readers.

Playlist

"Come Sail Away"
Styx

"ocean eyes"
Billie Eilish

"Crystal"
Fleetwood Mac
written by Stevie Nicks

"Only The Ocean"
Jack Johnson

"Blue Ocean Floor"
Justin Timberlake

"A Song I Heard the Ocean Sing"
Phish
Tom Marshall, lyricist

"This is the Sea"
The Waterboys

"If It's the Beaches"
Avett Brothers

"If I Had a Boat"
Lyle Lovett

"Wading in the Velvet Sea"
Phish
Tom Marshall, lyricist

Geezer Stories:
The Care and Feeding of Old People

The Narcissist's Wife

Also Available From

WordCrafts Press

Canelands
by Gerry Harlan Brown

Land That I Love
by Gail Kittleson

Gretchen and the Bear
by Carrie Anne Noble

Demimonde
by James E. Cressler

www.WordCrafts.net